BAD CALL

BAD CALL

STEPHEN WALLENFELS

HYPERION

LOS ANGELES NEW YORK

All rights reserved. Published by Hyperion, an imprint of Disney Book
Group. No part of this book may be reproduced or transmitted in any
form or by any means, electronic or mechanical, including photocopying,
recording, or by any information storage and retrieval system, without
written permission from the publisher. For information address
Hyperion, 125 West End Avenue, New York, New York 10023.

First Edition, December 2017
10 9 8 7 6 5 4 3 2 1
FAC-020093-17307

Printed in the United States of America

This book is set in 11-pt Adobe Caslon Pro, Adderville ITC Std, Futura LT
Pro, Goudy Modern MT Pro, New Century Schoolbook LT Pro/Monotype;
Full Tools Emoji Round Line, CoreCircus, KG All of Me/Fontspring

Designed by Whitney Manger Fine

Library of Congress Cataloging-in-Publication Data
Names: Wallenfels, Stephen, author.
Title: Bad call / Stephen Wallenfels.
Description: First edition. • Los Angeles : Hyperion, 2018. •
Summary: Four teenagers experience terrifying and unexpected
difficulties on a camping trip at Yosemite National Park.
Identifiers: LCCN 2017019209 (print) • LCCN 2016041770
(ebook) • ISBN 9781484780749 (ebook) • ISBN 9781484768136
(hardcover) • ISBN 1484768132 (hardcover)
Subjects: LCSH: Yosemite National Park (Calif.)—Fiction. •
CYAC: Yosemite National Park (Calif.)—Fiction. • Camping—Fiction.
• Hiking—Fiction. • Accidents—Fiction. • Survival—Fiction.
Classification: LCC PZ7.W158864 (print) • LCC
PZ7.W158864 Bad 2018 (ebook) • DDC [Fic]—dc23
LC record available at https://lccn.loc.gov/2017019209

Reinforced binding
Visit www.hyperionteens.com

SUSTAINABLE   Certified Sourcing
FORESTRY
INITIATIVE   www.sfiprogram.org
               SFI-00993

THIS LABEL APPLIES TO TEXT STOCK

To my mother, Mary, and my father, Otto

PROLOGUE

They walk side by side through shin-deep snow, dragging branches for their shelter behind them. The footprints they made on the way out are little more than small depressions in the drifts of swirling white. It's as if the wind has a single ill intent—to wipe out any traces of them.

"Did you bring your headlamp?" she asks.

"No. You?"

"No."

"We'll make it."

She wants to move faster, to outrun the dark that is chasing them, but knows each step is a struggle for him. The branches are too heavy. But she suspects the real problem is beyond her control. She can barely move her fingers in her gloves. His sneakers are caked in snow. His feet must be anchors of ice by now. She stops and faces him. "Let me carry more."

"Keep moving," he says.

"You sure? Because I can—"

"Must. Keep. Moving."

They trudge on, heads down into the stinging wind, following tracks that disappear before their eyes. She shudders as the nagging thought that was small thirty minutes ago swells into a chest-crushing wave of panic.

Are we walking in circles?

She decides to count. Numbers are a refuge, a singular focus that keeps her mind off the fear and pain. If we don't see the camp in fifty steps, I will tell him that we're lost.

She reaches thirty-eight when he points and says, "There it is."

She spots a small bubble of orange and yellow covered in white. The tent. A shape passes in front of it, hunched over, hat pulled down and covered with snow. Three steps, turn. Three steps, turn. He's pacing. At this distance she can't tell which one of them it is. A low moan rises up through the wind, rhythmic and throbbing.

"Something's wrong," he says.

As they move closer she recognizes the jacket.

Then she sees a big patch of black on the front that wasn't there when they left.

"What happened to his jacket?" she asks.

Her companion breaks into a run, goes three strides and falls facedown, scattering his load. He stands, takes two steps, falls again. She drops her branches, grabs his arm, and helps him up. They stumble together into camp, stop and stare in horror at the stain.

It's on his pants, his gloves, his face.

She knows in this dark moment what it is.

Her scream dies in the howling wind.

Clouds Rest

Mount
Watkins

SNOW CREEK

SNOW CREEK
FALLS

Tenaya Creek

FOOTBRIDGE

SNOW CREEK
FALLS TRAIL

Half Dome

MIRROR LAKE

North
Dome

YOSEMITE VALLEY

Merced River

Scale varies in this perspective view.
The distance from North Dome to
Mount Watkins is approximately
three miles.

THE DRIVE

1

COLIN

Backpacks on and racquet bags in hand, Grahame and I step out of the elevator in Darby Hall, arguing about a matter of great importance: who was better, Michael Jordan in 1995 or LeBron James after he won the NBA title with Miami in 2013. We walk across the lobby toward the front desk, Grahame saying, "Dude, LeBron is too big and too fast."

I answer, "But MJ never lost a championship final. He's six for six. Perfection is as perfection does."

Grahame says, "LeBron had more rings and MVPs than Jordan at the same age."

To which I respond, "But LeBron went into the NBA straight out of high school. He had a three-year head start."

We stop at the desk. So far, so good.

Grahame says, "What's your opinion, sir?"

Mr. Chetsanoyev, aka Mr. Chet, whose responsibility it is to make sure all forty-six students residing in Darby Hall don't get into any trouble between the hours of 10 p.m. and 7 a.m., looks up from his sudoku puzzle with unveiled suspicion. In his view, all students at Chandler Gates Academy are in constant escape mode, and he is the only wall of resistance preventing us from scoring our drugs and spiking the teen pregnancy rate. He takes in our geared-up backpacks and matching green-and-gold CGA TENNIS uniforms, and shakes his head. Whatever shenanigans we have planned will not work. We offer smiles, which he does not return. "LeBron has more triple-doubles," Grahame says to me, using the stylus to sign out on the registration iPad.

I say, "Jordan won defensive and offensive MVPs in the same season."

It's a fact I didn't know until last night.

Frowning at the iPad's display, Mr. Chet says, "A tournament in San Diego?"

"Yes, sir!" Grahame answers, with a heavy emphasis on *sir*. He had started addressing adults in this manner ever since deciding to be an Army Ranger, which he did after randomly meeting a recruiter in the Denver airport while traveling to Cape Cod to teach at a summer tennis camp for the über rich. Meanwhile I was flying back home to Vermont to count trout at a fish hatchery. Now he finishes every sentence to adults with *sir*, thinking it will prepare him for boot camp. And I swear my hands still smell like fish.

Mr. Chet asks, "Why are you leaving so early?"

"We want to beat the traffic, sir."

"At four a.m.?"

"There's always traffic in LA, sir."

"Is the whole team going?"

"No, sir! This is preseason. It's just us, plus Rhody and Ceo."

Mr. Chet smiles for the first time. This response is known as the Ceo Effect.

He says, "Is Coach Carson picking you up?"

"No, sir! Coach is in Boston at his niece's wedding. He won't be back till Tuesday."

"Till Tuesday, huh?"

"Correct, sir."

"Who's driving?"

"I am, sir."

"If you're playing in a tournament, then why the giant backpacks? Will you be climbing Everest between matches?" He smirks as if this question will be the one that trips us up. As if we'd forgotten about the packs. Grahame doesn't answer. Not because he doesn't have an answer lined up. It's because the ball is now in my court.

"We're camping in a nearby park," I say. My statement is mostly true. We will be camping, and we will be in a park. The nearby reference is relative. San Diego is three hundred miles from Yosemite and three thousand miles from Ball Mountain State Park in Vermont. Compare the two distances, and Yosemite qualifies as nearby. The flaw in this logic is that Mr. Chet may ask the name of the park, in which case I would be forced to tell a bald-faced lie. Ceo said the odds are four to one that he wouldn't ask that question. I have a name lined up, just in case.

"Hmmm, this looks pretty suspicious," Mr. Chet says, twisting the hairs in his beard. He rocks back in his chair and watches us watch him. What bugs me about this whole scenario is that we're all seniors. We should be able to do whatever the hell we want. But after some dismal scores on college placements, the Chandler Gates Academy board, commonly referred to as "the sacred six," made a highly contested policy that seniors may not go on extended weekend trips, as in more than one night, without parental and/or staff approval. The end result is we have to be more creative in how we get out the door. And no one is more creative than Ceo.

Mr. Chet shifts his gaze directly to me—the weakest link. Ceo anticipated this move because I'm the "honest" one. The guy least likely to break or even bend the rules. Not because I have a more highly evolved moral code. More like I'm the guy with the most to lose. One misstep and my "scholarship" is history. That was made abundantly clear during my interview with Coach Carson (one of the best in the country) and Maxine Taylor, the overlord of the Chandler Gates N-FAP (Needs-based Financial Assistance Package) treasure chest.

I brace myself for my next role in this mission.

"Colin," Mr. Chet says, "did Coach Carson sign off on this?"

"There's a note on the Need to Know page." Also true—sort of.

"Hmmmph." Mr. Chet frowns, rocks forward. Taps the display a couple of times. The changing screens flicker in his wire-framed glasses. Hopefully, Rhody got the upload done. He was scanning the revised version of Coach's note when we left his room last night. The revised version states we will be camping at a "nearby park" instead of what the original version from a different tournament states, which is we'll be staying at Ceo's father's guest condo in La Jolla. If Rhody didn't get that done, then we wind up playing tennis in LA smog instead of breathing the clean mountain air of Yosemite. I'd be okay if that happened. Make that *ecstatically* okay. But Mr. Chet settles on a page and reads the paragraph. If he were to look for this version in two hours, it would be gone. When he's finished, he says, "I think, given the actors involved, the best, ah, alternative, is for me to call Coach Carson."

Alternative is the word we were waiting for.

Grahame bumps me with an elbow.

I say, "That is one alternative. But it's seven a.m. in Boston, and Coach is jet-lagged. He needs his sleep for the big party."

"Well, I'm still not seeing a second alternative."

Grahame slips a small envelope out of his pocket and places it on the desk in a way that can't be seen by the security camera behind us. He nudges it forward and says in a near-whisper, "Here are four alternatives, sir."

Mr. Chet's eyes flick down, then up.

Grahame whispers, "Lakers versus Cavs."

"Same seats?"

"Better, sir. These are right behind the visitor bench."

Mr. Chet reaches out and tucks the envelope under his sudoku book. This action assures us that there will be no phone call to Coach and no follow-up phone call to Ceo's father, who is still in Tuscany buying wine for the cellar in their third home high on a cliff in Big Sur. And there will be no conversation with Coach about this conversation. Ever. If Coach wants to check online to see how we did in the tournament (which he won't, because it's small and not sanctioned), the link Rhody sent him will redirect him to a bogus page that shows the event was canceled due to lack of entries.

"Good luck in the tournament," Mr. Chet says.

We thank him and turn to leave. I'm reaching for the door when he says, "Tell Ceo that LeBron would eat Jordan for lunch and dinner."

"Roger that, sir!" Grahame says.

We step out into the cool morning air.

Phase One of Operation Cannabis Cove is in the bank.

We load our packs in the back of Grahame's aging Jeep Cherokee, then shed the uniforms down to our camping attire underneath. I noticed a shiny new ax in the rear compartment that wasn't there yesterday when we gassed up. Grahame must have made an extra trip to a hardware store. I think about asking him what's up with the ax, why not something lighter like a hatchet, but decide it's his business, not mine.

It takes a few cranks before the Cherokee shudders to life. Grahame guns the engine till the idle settles, finds the dreaded Road Trip playlist on his Samsung and cranks it up. We roar out of the parking lot vibrating to the thumping bass of Bob Marley telling us all to be happy. It's a three-minute drive to Larner Hall if you honor the speed bumps behind the library and don't cut across the PE parking lot. Grahame does it in two. Between impacts he says in his bogus Jamaican accent, because that's how he rolls when he be crankin' da reggae, mon, "Are ya sure about dis ting, Q?"

"I'm sure."

"Ya deedn't look so sure last night."

"I was tired."

Dropping the accent, he says, "I'd still be pissed if I was you."

"I'm not *still* pissed."

He looks at me, frowns. "Then what are you?"

"I'm . . . transitioning."

He grunts, *Bullshit,* makes a screeching left into the Larner Hall parking lot. Ceo is under a streetlamp, leaning against his red Mercedes convertible, sending a text.

Grahame says, "But cha won't be sleepin een da Ceo's tent, eh, mon?"

"Roger that," I say.

2

COLIN

Grahame pulls into the parking space next to Ceo's car, guns the engine to keep it from stalling. Ceo pockets his phone, which has me wondering, Who is he texting at 4:15 a.m.? I get out, slip the *Good Will Hunting* screenplay out of my pack. I ask Ceo if he'd like shotgun, thinking I'd rather read about an undiscovered Einstein in Boston for the third time than listen to Grahame talk about one of the many girls he had "privileges" with while teaching backhands at camp Rich 'n' Famous. Ceo says, nah, he's going to sit behind Grahame, then whispers to me, "That way I can strangle him if he talks in that freaking accent." He loads his backpack in the rear compartment with the rest of our gear, takes a moment rooting around, then climbs into the backseat.

"Hit it," Ceo says.

Grahame pumps the gas. The Cherokee spews a cloud of black smoke but we don't move.

"Works better if you put it in *D* for *drive*," Ceo says.

"There's an empty seat," Grahame says.

"Is there? I hadn't noticed."

"Where's your flaky roommate?"

"Flaking."

"What?" Grahame stares bullets at Ceo in the rearview mirror.

"He isn't coming."

"Since when?"

"Since twenty minutes ago when I said get your geeky ass out of bed and he said my geeky ass is staying here."

This is news of the worst kind. Rhody is the only person on the team, Coach included, who can keep our undisputed alpha males from going nuclear. He's like the team rodeo clown, hence the name Rhody, along with the convenient fact that he's from Rhode Island. Without him as a buffer, all the pressure falls squarely on me. Plus, I don't see the point of rodeos, and clowns are straight-up evil.

I say to Ceo, "Why the change of heart?"

"The usual Rhody bullshit. Too many tests, too little time."

"You reminded him that this is a sacred poker vow?" Grahame asks.

"Absolutely. He was stressing a couple days ago. I told him that this isn't just a camping trip. It's a pilgrimage. I thought that settled him down. But you know how he gets."

Grahame looks at me. I shrug. It's widely known that if Rhody had to choose between an emergency splenectomy and risking the loss of his lifetime 4.0, he'd sacrifice his spleen and go for the GPA. On the other hand, Ceo can talk a turtle out of its shell. This isn't a case of an irresistible force meeting an immovable object. Rhody would cave. We all cave in the presence of Ceo. Rhody wanted to go on this trip and now he isn't. Something smells fishy. And if anyone knows what fishy smells like, it's me.

Grahame pounds the steering wheel. "Well, sheet, mon. Who's gonna pay hees share uv da gas, because me don't wanna be doin' dat, don't cha know."

"Q," Ceo says. "Translate whatever the hell your roommate just said."

Ceo knows exactly what Grahame said, but I play along anyway. It's the path of least resistance. I say, "He wants to know who's going to pay Rhody's share of the gas."

Ceo opens his wallet, peels a fifty off a thick wad of bills, slaps it on the center armrest next to Grahame. "I'll cover his gas."

"Ah don't know, mon," Grahame says, eyes on the crisp bill. "We be three people instead of dah four. Dees blows da whole fookin' deal, don't cha know."

Ceo leans back, tilts his Dodgers ball cap low over his eyes. "I'm working on a new fookin' deal."

Grahame gives me a querying look, says, "What do you think?"

As if I have a clue about what goes on in Ceo's head. If Grahame had asked me fifteen days ago, then yeah, I would have shared my opinion. But that was before the challenge match. Before Ceo scorch-earthed our friendship and left me and my future swinging in the breeze. Now it's a struggle to muster up the will to care. I say, "Your car. Your call."

He takes a moment, slips the fifty into his pocket.

Steps on da fookin' gas.

3

COLIN

Operation Cannabis Cove requires one stop before we leave town—Big O Donuts for breakfast. They have the undisputed best donuts on the planet, and you can buy a dozen for $2.99 between four and four thirty. We make the cutoff with two minutes to spare. Grahame loses the three-way coin flip and gets the honors. While he's inside, Ceo asks me if there were any problems with Mr. Chet.

"None," I say. "You?"

"All good."

"Except Rhody."

"Except him." The backseat goes quiet, probably because he's checking his phone. He mutters, *Shit,* then asks, "Did Mr. Chet like the package?"

"He did."

"The Jordan versus LeBron thing worked?"

"As advertised. But I thought you were only doing two tickets."

"I figured a little extra insurance wouldn't hurt."

I wonder about the cost of that extra insurance, do the mental math, and come up with a number exceeding what I make in three months folding towels. Then I wonder how Ceo scored the tickets in the first place. I could ask him. But I don't bother because he'd just say something evasive like *Craigslist is a gift from God*, or cryptic like *I know a guy that knows a guy*. We watch Grahame pay the cashier, then head for the door with a box of pastries in hand.

Ceo asks, "Are you curious about my new plan?"

"Not especially."

"I think you should ask me about it."

I'm really not in the mood, but I say, "Okay, what's the new plan?"

"It's still forming. But you're going to like it more than the old plan."

"What about Grahame?"

"That wheel's going to need some extra grease."

Somehow he manages to be evasive *and* cryptic.

Grahame opens the door, digs out a donut, hands the box back to Ceo. Just as the Cherokee is turning right onto Nelson Ave., heading for the highway out of town, an irritated voice out of the dark behind us says, "Dude, what the hell?"

"What's wrong?" Grahame asks.

"They're all maple bars!"

"You wanted a dozen donuts, I got a dozen donuts."

"This isn't a dozen donuts. This is the same freaking donut twelve times."

Ceo has a lot of secrets. More than anyone I know. One of those secrets is not his open disgust for any food with maple in or on it. On the day we met he told me he would never go to Vermont just because of all the maple trees.

Grahame takes a shark-size bite out of his pastry and asks, "How's da new plan workin' for ya now, chief?"

Ceo doesn't talk for thirty minutes. I think he's asleep back there with his hat so low it rests on his nose. Grahame consumes three maple bars while asking me sample questions from the ASVAB, which he'll be taking in two weeks and expects to pass with scores that will qualify him for a signing bonus big enough to retire this piece of shit Cherokee. Then out of the blue Ceo, with the hat still down low, says, "I need someone to answer a question for me."

"What question?" Grahame asks.

"Why is there an ax in the trunk?"

"I thought it might be useful."

"Useful how?"

"You think we might want to cut some firewood?"

"You think it might be a little heavy?"

Grahame turns up the music.

Ceo raises the hat a quarter inch, says over the noise, "Dude. You're joking, right?"

No response from Grahame.

Ceo says, "Tell me you're not seriously thinking about hauling a freaking *fifteen-pound ax* on a *twenty-mile hike*?"

Grahame grins into the rearview, says, "I wasn't."

4

COLIN

Ceo insists we take a pee break at the Quick-Stop in Caruthers. He says he saw an image on Google Earth, and this may be the coolest roadside convenience store we'll ever see. He may be right. It has an actual crashed plane sticking tail-up from the canopy over the pumps. While Grahame tops off the tank, Ceo asks me to snap a picture with his phone of him pretending to balance the plane in his palm. Then Ceo and I cruise the Quick-Stop, searching out Mike and Ikes for me and Red Bulls for him and Grahame. We're in the process of doing all that and thinking the JoJos just out of the fryer smell pretty damn good when the door chimes.

And a girl walks in.

She's tanned and fit in a personal trainer kind of way. I'd put her in college or just out, wearing a blue dress with flowers on the front, not quite reaching midthigh, and shoes with heels, like she's on her way to a real job. Definitely well within Ceo range, who claims to have scored all the way up to his Spanish tutor, who is forty-one. She pushes her sunglasses up onto shimmering black hair and surveys the aisles. Probably stopped here for coffee, or maybe a new key chain for the white Lexus sedan she parked next to the door.

Her gaze inevitably lands on Ceo, who was in the process of buying the Red Bulls, but now he's not.

It's like watching reruns on the nature channel. Instead of the Quick-Stop, we're at a dusty watering hole in the African savanna. The narrator whispers: *"The male wildebeest sniffs the air, stomps his foot, and snorts. The female wildebeest responds by turning slightly away before twitching her tail, then tentatively steps closer. . . ."*

Ceo laughs whenever I tell him this. Says I'm overestimating the Ceo Effect. The sad truth is there could be a party full of males and females talking and having fun. Enter one chisel-chinned Ceo with that sun-kissed surfer hair, fitness-model abs, and carefully groomed stubble making him look three years older than he really is, and all the other males turn into slobbering warthogs. I know this as a fact because I've turned into a warthog so many times I'm growing tusks.

And that is exactly what happens now. In fact, she almost bumps into me and my box of candy on her way to the refrigerator, suddenly remembering she needs a pint of half-and-half to go with the coffee she forgot to buy. She opens the cooler door next to Ceo. Says something to him that rewards her with an easy Ceo smile. He holds the door while she reaches up and up to get a carton of something—I don't know what because her legs are distracting me, and I've witnessed Ceo in this dance too many times.

I head for the register, hoping that I don't impale any customers on my tusks.

Grahame and I are leaning back against the Cherokee, chewing Mike and Ikes under that crashed plane when Ceo and the girl walk out of the Quick-Stop laughing and bumping shoulders. Ceo holds the driver's door while she folds her legs into the Lexus. He lingers on the view before closing the door. The tinted window glides down and a hand floats out with a piece of paper. Ceo pockets it as she drives away.

With the sated wildebeest walking toward us, Grahame says to me, "Dude's a freak of nature."

"He does possess special powers."

"But at a Quick-Stop? In freaking Caruthers?"

"There is no immunity on planet Ceo."

Grahame shakes his head. "You know. Sometimes. Sometimes I just wish..."

I wait for him to finish that thought. Part of me hopes he doesn't because there's a layer of darkness underneath it that I'm pretty sure I don't want to hear. On the other hand, maybe I do.

Ceo stops. Checks his phone. Smiles, thumbs a text.

Grahame, back on to that other thing, says, "Why'd you let him win?"

Here we go again. Ceo is walking toward us now. I have ten seconds to respond to a question that would take three hours to answer and still get wrong.

All I say is, "We've addressed this topic."

"And your answer still sucks."

"For the last time. And I mean the *last time*. I didn't let him win."

"Dat's de same answer, mon."

"So change the question."

"You totally tanked the match, Q. I saw the shot."

When Grahame gets onto something, it's hard to get him off. He plays tennis that way, relentless and focused, like a pit bull on a leg bone. When he smells blood—forget about it. You may as well pack up your shit and go home. I know he won't give up on this particular subject until he hears the truth. The problem is I can't tell him what I don't know. I keep reminding myself that it's just a line call in a match that when compared to bigger deals like climate change and Ebola, doesn't matter any more than the box of candy in my hand. So I shake out a piece. It's cherry red. I show it to Grahame and ask, "Is this a Mike or an Ike? They don't tell you which is which on the box. It's a mystery. Why don't you ask me *that* question?"

Grahame frowns. "He don't deserve it, mon."

"Doesn't deserve what?"

There's no time for an answer because Ceo walks up to us, trying hard to contain a smile. "Let's roll, dudes," he says. "We have another stop to make."

"Where to now, chief?" Grahame asks.

Ceo's smile breaks loose. It outshines the sun.

"The Fresno airport."

With the crashed plane fading in our rearview mirror and Ceo rapid-firing texts in the backseat, Grahame looks at me and says, "Eets your undying affection, mon. Dat's what."

He studies his friend on the other side of the net. Stooped shoulders, T-shirt soaked, panting like a sled dog—Ceo is a broken man. It started when Ceo's backhand, which is usually solid, went MIA late in the first set tiebreaker. Colin won the set, 7–6. Ever since then he's picked on Ceo's backhand like a crow on a carcass. He knew if the situation were reversed, as it was in the previous match, Ceo would do the same thing. Colin tosses the ball high into the LA sun and serves to Ceo's backhand. Ceo shanks the return wide.

Match point.

Colin lines up for his next serve, checks on Ceo to make sure he's ready. It's a predator-prey moment, and this time Colin is not the prey. But in that moment he sees something that hasn't been there before, an intensity in Ceo's eyes that startles him even from seventy-eight feet away. Dark and threatening, like if Colin dares to win this point, this match—he will be crossing a new and different line. For reasons he still doesn't understand, Colin backs off.

He serves to Ceo's forehand, his money shot, instead of his bleeding backhand. They have an exchange of crosscourt ground strokes. Even presented with opportunities to attack, Colin refuses to hit to Ceo's backhand. After the tenth shot, Ceo hits a forehand short, and Colin approaches the net, forcing Ceo to hit a forehand passing shot that on a normal day he could make with his eyes closed. But today is not a normal day. It lands wide. The margin is a half inch at most. Colin sees it land clearly outside the line and makes the call.

The match is over. Colin wins.

Ceo storms the net, screaming like a banshee that Colin hooked him. That the shot was clearly in. He slams his racquet on the net, then the ground, shattering the frame. He turns and hurls the mangled racquet over the fence. It lands on top of the PE building. By this time all the players on the other courts have stopped their games. They watch this display of pure, unfiltered rage. As Colin stands at the net, stunned beyond speaking, he wonders if hatred is boiling in there, too. And if it is, where did it come from?

He tells Ceo, I saw the shot out.

Ceo says, So that's your call?

Colin says, Yes, that's my call.

Ceo says, Well, then you hooked me, Q. I can't believe it. My best friend cheats me on match point.

Shaking now, Colin says, I didn't cheat. But if you want, we can replay the point.

Ceo says, No, that was a bad call. What I want is for you to do the right thing and fucking change it.

Colin blinks, says nothing.

Ceo walks to the bench, hauls a new racquet out of his bag, and stomps back to receive serve. He shakes his head, muttering expletives all the way, as if this is the greatest injustice in the history of sports. Colin can't believe what he's seeing. All Ceo has riding on this match is a chance to play Grahame for the number one spot. For Colin it means he would drop out of the top two and probably lose his scholarship. But seeing his friend like this flips a switch in Colin's will to win. He double-faults the next two points, loses the game and every game after that until his death spiral is complete. They meet at the net. Ceo offers his hand to shake; Colin doesn't take it.

Ceo says, You played tough, Q.

Colin is too numb to speak.

They walk to their separate benches, pack up their gear in silence.

Colin leaves for the locker room first.

Ceo calls out, Q, I'm sorry. I saw what I saw.

Colin, because it's the only response that comes to mind, raises an arm and extends his middle finger.

5

ELLIE

Three Days Earlier

They sit at their favorite table in the corner with poor lighting but an excellent view of the tattooed barista when he's working the drive-thru. Ellie sipping green tea with organic honey from local bees, Nadia cradling a variant of coffee topped with caramel-striped foam. Ellie has big news to share but must wait because Nadia launches first, saying that AP Chem is way harder than she thought it would be. Dropping it may be her only choice if she wants to have a life, but Vanessa told her no way she'll get into Berkeley or any UC school for that matter without at least three AP classes, so what to do, what to do? Ellie assures her that Ms. Callaway does this every year to scare off the poseurs. Just never ever skip the labs, when in doubt choose *C*, and laugh every time she says, "Hey, kiddos! Matter matters!" Ellie advises Nadia to drop Eric Westerman instead of AP Chem because then you *will* have a life *and* a future, and anyway he so richly deserves it. Then Nadia says, "How did you take AP Chem as a sophomore and still get a four-point? Who, like, does that anyway?"

Ellie asks, "We're on me now?"

"Sure. But why am I getting that look?"

"What look?"

"The look mothers have when they think their teenage daughter is pregnant."

"Maybe you know that look, but I don't."

"So why did you buy my drink? You never buy my drink."

"I have pictures to share."

Nadia puts down her coffee. Ellie calls up a website on her phone, swipes to the page, and gives her phone to Nadia, who stares in unrestrained admiration. Ellie can't blame her. Whoever took the pic was very good. She would have adjusted the shutter speed up a little bit, and the framing could be better—the lifeguard tower in the background is unnecessary clutter and should have been photoshopped out. But the lighting is perfect. The contrast between sun and shadow, combined with a golden dusting of sand in just the right places, captured each straining muscle in rippled perfection. His tanned face, with high prominent cheekbones and angular jawline, makes him look older than his seventeen years. And his eyes, a little on the narrow side, create a sense of burning intensity. It's as if the camera lens clicking at seven frames per second didn't exist and there was nothing more urgent than going horizontal to catch a yellow Frisbee.

Nadia, eyes still on the screen, says, "Who is he?"

"Ceo DeVrees."

"The guy you hung out with at the workshop?"

"Theater arts workshop. But yes, he's the one."

"The one with the famous father?"

"That's him."

"You said he played tennis at CGA. And that he did some modeling. But you never said he was this…"

"This what?"

"This good at catching Frisbees." Nadia swipes to another picture, then another. Fans her face. "I mean, like, holy mother of freaking shit!" Her outburst earns an over-the-laptop raised eyebrow from the guy at the next table.

Ellie says, "That's enough stimulation for you," and pries her phone from Nadia's reluctant fingers.

Nadia says, "But that was in June."

"One hundred and twenty-six days ago."

"Ooooh. Someone has secrets."

Ellie sips her tea, holds back a smile.

"Someone is a sly little minx!"

"We were texting but not *that* kind of texting. Four or five times a day at first—then four or five times a week. Then hardly any in August. I sent a couple texts after school started, but he didn't reply. I figured he had moved on, so I did too. And then this morning"—Ellie calls up another screen on her phone and hands it back to Nadia—"I get this."

CEO

Hey Cusey! Do you still like camping?

Nadia looks up. "Cusey?"

"Not relevant. Keep reading."

ELLIE

Conditionally.

CEO

I will be in Yosemite this weekend with friends. Can u come?

Pls say yes.

Unconditionally.

Nadia tries to scroll further, but the conversation ends. She returns the phone to Ellie. Sits back in her chair and says after a few moments, "Someone wants to play Frisbee with you."

"It's not like that. We were—or at least I thought we were—really good friends."

"*Camping? In Yosemite?* That's Frisbee code, Els!"

Ellie stares at the green remnants of her tea.

Nadia says, "Did you answer him?"

"No."

"You're revenge-ignoring him?"

"No."

"Because?"

"I'm conflicted."

"Aha! So that's why you paid for my drink. You want me to de-conflict you!"

"If that was a real word. But more like I want you to set the process in motion."

"Okay. I can do that." Nadia takes a thoughtful sip. "Are you ready to start?"

"Yes."

"First question. Do you trust him?"

"Your version of trust or mine?"

"We're on you now."

"In that case, yes. I trust him."

"Why?"

"Like I previously stated. We're friends."

"With or without benefits?"

Ellie takes a long beat. "Next question."

"Ho-kay." Nadia carves a check mark in the air. "I'll put that in the *N* folder for no benefits. Unless you want to explain." And sips again. All she gets from across the table is blank-faced silence. "All right, then. Moving on. Mr. Frisbee's text said 'this weekend.' Does that mean a sleepover?"

"I assume so."

"What are the sleeping arrangements?"

"I don't know."

Nadia carves another check mark. "That goes in the *B* folder for bullshit. My next-to-last question: Who are his friends?"

Ellie thinks about the friends Ceo made at the workshop and discounts them right away. He didn't connect with any guys because they were all jealous of the attention he got from the girls, and she doubted he would be asking more than one female on a camping trip, although she could think of two at the workshop that would say yes without thinking twice. The only friends Ceo talked about with her were on the tennis team at CGA, and only one that he mentioned more than once. That friend was from Vermont, and Ceo referred to him as "Q." The team picture on the website listed one guy from Vermont. His name was Colin. He looked vaguely familiar, but she couldn't figure out how. Still, Ellie decides to answer Nadia's question with the simple truth: "I don't know."

"You don't know who his friends are?"

"Correct."

"So, technically speaking, this camping trip could be an invitation to a *sausage fest*?"

"It could. But it's not."

"And you know this how?"

"I defer to answer number one."

Nadia has to think. She says, "You *trust* him?"

"I do."

"Holy shit! You need a better answer than that. I mean, seriously better. Because the Ellie I know, the one who scored 2200 on the SAT and has colleges flying her to see them, that Ellie wouldn't waste two seconds on this guy. Sure, he has great abs. Amazing abs, actually. I'd date those abs. But the Ellie I know doesn't date body parts, unless it's the brain. And Mr. Frisbee didn't get those ripples reading science books. So, tell me, whoever you are sitting across from me drinking that tea, W. T. F.?"

Ellie looks at the tattooed barista. Rumor has it he has a law degree from Loma Linda and passed the bar two years ago. Was married, divorced, maybe has a kid in another state, and flew helicopters in Iraq. Yet here he is, leaning out the drive-thru window, putting on a show for the girls at the register. Rumor also has it he's starting up a band.

Ellie says, "Newton's first law."

"What?"

"Newton's first law."

"Newton? Is he the guy that says stupid shit will happen because people are stupid?"

"That's Murphy—in a vaguely inaccurate *Wikipedia*-ish sort of way. Newton was a seventeenth-century physicist."

"Can I get an answer that doesn't involve science?"

"Not my fault you dropped physics."

"Fine. Be like that. Here's my last question. What's up with Cusey?"

"That's him making fun of my thing for John Cusack."

"Oooh, I like him already." Nadia sits back in her chair, studies Ellie from a distance. Then she nods at the tattooed barista. "Buy me another cup of whatever. And an almond scone, but make sure he nukes it. He always does a little dance when he nukes stuff."

"I know it well."

"Oh, and leave your phone. Before passing judgment, I need to see those abs again."

Ellie leaves her phone. When she returns, Nadia is waiting, her face dangerously unreadable. The phone is screen down on the table.

"Well?" Ellie asks.

"Sir Isaac Newton discovered gravity."

"You googled him?"

"I did."

"So," Ellie says, sinking into her chair, trying to read that face and not liking what she doesn't see, "how shall I proceed?"

"You don't proceed."

"Okay." And feels a wave of something she hopes is relief.

"Because," Nadia says, looking at Ellie's phone, "I proceeded for you."

"What does that mean?"

The phone dings.

After the ding fades, "Oh, shit. Nadia, you didn't. Please tell me you didn't!"

Nadia smiles.

Ellie snatches up her phone. Heart thumping, she stares at the screen.

ELLIE

> Absofreakinglutely. Bring your Frisbee. Let's play.

CEO

> Yeefreakingha! Frisbee is packed and good to go.

6

ELLIE

Ellie says, "Want to know where I went this weekend?" and dives right. She catches the soccer ball three feet off the ground in her outstretched goalie-gloved hands, lands hard on the grass in front of the goal, which after twenty minutes of this abuse is more mud than grass. She leaps to her feet, rolls the ball to Nadia, who stops it with a cleated foot.

Nadia, with a dozen soccer balls scattered around her, says, "Of course I do. Where *did* you go this weekend?" She kicks the ball hard and low to Ellie's left.

Ellie dives, makes the saving catch, rolls the ball to Nadia. "I flew to LA, got picked up by Jenny, and she gave me a tour of the Pepperdine campus."

"Pepperdine is on your short list?"

"No. But it's on my father's. The helpful people in Malibu said if I ever wanted to see the campus, just give them a call. So I called."

"Your parents were okay with you going alone?"

"My dad is in Seattle presenting at an oncology conference. Mom is driving my sister everywhere as usual. Then she has to prep for a case. They told me to make the right choices."

"Lucky you."

"The stars appear to be aligning."

"Who's Jenny?" Nadia tees up another penalty kick.

"Jenny from admissions. She's perky and blond and looks remarkably like someone I cropped out of a stock photo. And future Nadia was very helpful, by the way."

"That was nice of me. What did future Nadia do?" Nadia drills a shot at Ellie's torso. She catches the ball, stumbles backward a step from the impact, fires an overarm pass to Nadia, who executes a perfect chest trap.

Ellie says, "You tweeted a couple pictures on my account with *#lovin' the pdine* and *#go waves!*, which you of course retweeted to everyone. Then you posted a selfie of me and Jenny in front of the Odell McConnell Law Center on my Instagram and Facebook, which you promptly liked and shared with everyone."

"You hate selfies."

"True. Almost as much as any movie with Seann William Scott. But my mom appreciated it. She says your Facebook page is better than mine, by the way."

"That's because your Facebook page is a John Cusack stalker site that you clutter up with quotes from old movies that no one watches. So where did I get the bogus pictures I haven't seen yet?" Nadia jukes left, then chips a high kick toward the upper-right corner. Ellie barely makes the save, finger-tipping the ball so it sails over the goal by inches.

"I finished photoshopping them later tonight, then handed them to you on a flash drive tomorrow morning, when you gave me a ride to the airport."

"Future Nadia gave you a ride to the airport?"

"Wasn't that nice of her?"

"Too nice. Why?"

"Because my mother would wonder why I'm taking a huge backpack to Pepperdine."

"Oh, right. So...like, what time did I give you this ride?"

A whistle blows in the background. A female voice calls out, "Five more minutes, everyone. Then corner kicks before sprints. Monica! Stop dribbling and cross the ball!"

Ellie says, "My flight left at eight fifteen. You picked me up at five fifty. And for once you weren't late."

"Five fifty? In the *A* freaking *M*? Future Nadia is a better friend than I thought."

"She felt guilty because it's her freaking fault that I'm in this mess."

"As she recalls, you thanked her on Monday."

"I doubted that."

Nadia places the ball on the penalty mark. "How did you pay for the ticket without your mom knowing?"

"I didn't."

"Who did?"

Ellie pretends to throw a Frisbee.

"Seriously?"

"The man has resources."

Nadia grins. "You got that right."

Coach yells, "Nadia! I don't see any balls in the net! Less talking, more scoring!"

Nadia backs up, points to the goal. "Sorry, Els. This one is going in."

"Nope. It wants to be with all its loser friends." Ellie nods behind the goal to a dozen soccer balls scattered like oversize marbles in the grass. She goes into a crouch, hands forward, fingers spread and curved just a little. Her eyes focused like twin lasers on Nadia's right foot.

Nadia says, "Don't forget to pee right after you get off the plane."

"Why?"

"Because I hear they sell condoms in the restrooms at Fresno."

Nadia runs and kicks.

Ellie dives right, punches the ball into tomorrow.

7

ELLIE

S he watches the gray pavement rush toward them, then turn into a gray blur. Ellie waits for that breathless moment when gravity overcomes lift and the landing gear reassuringly thumps. After the brakes engage and the plane slows to a survivable speed, she finally exhales. The man next to her, who hogged the armrest without remorse, pulls out his phone. She does the same. A text is waiting.

CEO

U there yet?

ELLIE

Almost to the gate.

I hope your plane landed better than this one.

She smiles at the bizarre image of Ceo holding a crashed plane, stubbed out like a cigarette, in the palm of his hand.

ELLIE

> That IS my plane!
> Where are you?

CEO

> Almost there. We'll see you soon.

Not *I'll* see you soon.

We'll.

Making sure she remembers that he isn't alone.

As if that wasn't one of three concerns occupying her thoughts as she sipped V8 juice at twenty-eight thousand feet and hoped that the more-than-occasional turbulence was not a metaphor for events to follow. First on the list was how her parents would react after the inescapable discovery that she didn't go to Pepperdine. That she went camping in Yosemite instead and used a variety of elaborate deceptions to make it possible, including the duplicitous corruption (the words her father would most likely use) of her best friend, Nadia. The fact that it was with a guy, and even worse, a guy that they didn't know, will be a force multiplier with an X potential that will lead to a highly predictable outcome. An outcome that has been in the wings but whose time has definitely come.

Second on the list was how the reunion with Ceo would play out at the airport. She wasn't sure where her emotions would land on a scale ranging from extreme disappointment that he ignored her for so long to her heart racing just like it did when they almost kissed at the beach in June. Being stuck in *almost* for so long, then moving on, then being pulled back in has a pain potential she'd rather not assign a value.

Last on the list, but not far behind number two, is the *we'll* in this equation. Who are they, and which side of the equation will she be on? Of all the variables, the friend question is the most knowable. Because now she has a clue.

Ellie studies the picture as the plane taxies to the gate. Ceo, prominent in the foreground, looks as good as ever. His hair is a little longer than she remembers, and maybe a little blonder. There's a Quick-Stop convenience store in the far distance. The middle distance is where she spends her time. A green SUV has a hose sticking out of the tank. Leaning back against the SUV is a guy in a black T-shirt and jeans, facing them, arms folded across his chest. His hair is short, black or dark brown, and he looks like he's about their age, with heavy features that make him appear closer to eighteen than seventeen. By using the pumps for reference, she can tell that he's big, definitely an inch or possibly two over six feet, and that his chest is nearly as wide as the pumps. His arms make the gas hose look like a piece of twine. She zooms in on his face. It's darkened by shadows and badly pixelated, so the details are sketchy. It is longish and narrow, a sharp contrast to the rest of him. The eyes are black smudges, so no help there. The only point of absolute clarity are his lips. Shaped like a smile, but not amused. Closer to bored, like *here we go again*. Her photography instincts tell her that there is more to read if she wants to take the time. Which she doesn't. The overall effect is unsettling, and she pockets her phone.

As the plane rolls to a stop and the door opens she considers the final unknown. Who took the picture? If the big guy by the pumps is part of the group, and because of his age she thinks he is, logic would indicate that to balance the equation the gender of the photographer must be female. Maybe the big guy's girlfriend? But balance is relative and easily lost. And logic, she reminds herself, went out the window when Ceo sent his text three days ago.

Ellie makes her way through the terminal, stops to admire the faux forest-theme decor along the way. By the time she reaches baggage claim the conveyor belt for her flight is turning and scattered with luggage. Her backpack isn't among them. She searches the room, and Ceo isn't there.

Her phone dings.

NADIA

Frisbee update ☺

ELLIE

No F in sight.

NADIA

You land in LA in
ten minutes.

ELLIE

Am I crazy?

☺

She searches for Ceo again, comes up empty. The crowd is thinning, and so are the bags. Ellie resigns herself to counting the seconds per revolution of the conveyor belt while weighing the pros and cons of her backpack being lost. She determines the results are equivalent to a coin flip.

Her phone dings again. Nadia is enjoying this way too much.

CEO

What's up?

ELLIE

I'm watching luggage go
round and round.

CEO

Sounds like fun.

ELLIE

For the luggage. RU close?

Very.

How very?

Is that your backpack making babies with a green duffel?

Ellie looks up, sees a green Adidas duffel bag on top of her pack. She spins, searches the faces of the remaining passengers. Finds him leaning against the wall under the Men's Restroom sign. *How long has he been there?* Nadia would laugh at the symbolism of this location. Ceo waves; his face spreads into a smile.

Well, she thinks as he pushes off and starts walking her way, *one of the variables is solved.*

X = racing heart.

8

ELLIE

He wraps his arms around her, and all the pieces are there. Lean and rippled under his T-shirt. Familiar scents of herbal shampoo, coconut, plus the undertones of emerging sweat.

But.

There's a distance in his embrace. A subtle but certain gap. The pieces are here, she thinks, but they aren't fitting.

Ceo releases her and steps back. Sweeps her with those too-green eyes. "Your hair's shorter."

"Soccer season. It's my warrior look."

"I like it."

Then his gaze shifts beyond her and starts tracking right to left. She turns in time to see a woman in a ridiculously tight blue dress stop at the exit and give Ceo an over-the-shoulder glance before walking out the door. Ellie, keenly aware of her own khaki trail shorts, wool socks, and Gore-Tex trekking shoes, says, "You like that warrior look better."

"Nah," Ceo says, "she wouldn't last a mile in those heels."

His bemused expression reminds her of what it was like at the theater arts workshop, the constant flirting from the other girls, their incredulous looks when he asked her in front of them to be his partner for the final project. But that lighter-than-air moment turned into a chain of unanswered texts, bruised pride—and a spur-of-the-moment haircut. She wants to ask, *Do you have actual relationships, or do women just orbit you like planets around the sun?* Yet here she is, standing in front of him at the Fresno airport.

Ceo says, "You ready to be a happy camper?"

"Yes."

"Good. I'll get your pack. Then it's time to meet the guys."

As he heads for the conveyor belt Ellie says, "Excuse me. Did you say '*guys*'?"

9

ELLIE

She spots them in an idling SUV twenty feet from the door. There are two, sitting in the front seat. Recognizes the driver as the big guy from Ceo's text, the one that was pumping gas. Ellie takes out her phone and thumbs a text to Nadia.

ELLIE

> When is next flight
> to SF?

Ceo, out the door, a few seconds behind her says, "What's wrong?"

"That." Ellie pushes send, points to the green SUV parked in the handicapped zone.

"You don't like the ride? It's a classic."

"I don't like the balance."

"What balance?"

"You're serious?"

"Yes."

"Three parts testosterone, one part estrogen."

"Oh, *that* balance."

"Yeah, that balance."

NADIA

In class. WTF?

He says, "I told you there would be friends."

"You should have told me they were all guys."

"But these are tennis players. They're basically like Smurfs."

NADIA

On it.

Ellie senses him moving closer. Into her personal space. She tries to focus on Nadia's text, how to purchase the ticket without her parents knowing, but can't make the information resolve into a meaningful thought.

He says, "What are you doing?"

"Buying a flight home."

"Don't do that."

"Why not?"

"I have a better idea."

NADIA

12:50. American. $460

She looks at him. Hopes he sees the smoldering wreckage of this weekend in her eyes.

Ceo says, "It's a two-hour drive to the park entrance. Ride with us that far. When we get there I'll ask you a question about Smurfs. If you say you like them, then we keep going. If you say you don't like Smurfs, or that they're stupid, or the wrong color or whatever, then I'll drop my friends off at the trailhead, and you and I can do our own thing."

"Define own thing."

"Whatever you want it to be."

"What if I don't feel comfortable with you?"

"Won't happen."

"Sorry. That object is already in motion."

"Then I'll drive you home. Or back to the airport. Whatever you want."

NADIA

Book it?

Ellie shows him the text. "My friend is ready to buy the ticket."

Ceo says, "Tell her to save her money. Please."

She turns from him, looks at the SUV. The big guy doesn't move. But the passenger sitting next to him smiles and waves. Ellie recognizes him from the website. That must be Q. But she can't get over the feeling that she's seen him before, at a different time in a different context.

Ceo says, "C'mon. It'll be a great weekend. Mountains, fresh air. Smurfs."

The SUV guns its engine.

She says, "We'll do our own thing?"

"Whatever you want."

"Just to be clear, I hate Smurfs. They're creepier than clowns."

Ceo smiles while she sends the text.

ELLIE

False alarm. All good.

His father says, I have one more present for you. Slips an envelope from under his sweater and hands it to Colin. The flap is torn and resealed with Scotch tape. Colin stares at his father's writing in black Sharpie on the front.

For a Sole Emergency

They had already given him $825 in twenties, tens, fives, and ones. It's the cash his mother saved by not smoking for two years, which she was squirreling away for a new leather sofa, maybe even a sectional. But *she would never tell him that—not even on her deathbed with angels swirling around.*

He asks, Should I open it now or later?

Now is good, his father says.

Colin wonders if he has the time to do this. The security line is pretty short. Two minutes at most. The Burlington airport hums around them with early-morning travelers on cell phones rolling their luggage across polished tile floors. He inches forward and adds his bit to the muted din.

Chop-chop, his father says.

Colin carefully peels back the tape and opens the envelope. There's a gift card for fifty dollars to Foot Locker inside.

It's for a new pair of tennis sneakers when those wear out.

Thanks, Colin says, this is perfect. He doesn't say that his Nikes wore out two months ago and the fifty dollars would buy one shoe, not a pair. He knows what his father is giving up with this gift. Probably means no studs for the tires this winter.

His father says to save it for a big match.

Colin says they're all big.

His father guarantees that some are bigger than others.

The TSA agent nods at Colin.

Colin's father gives him a long hug. Stands back and watches while he hands the TSA agent his ID and ticket, one-way to LAX via Detroit, arriving at 2:48 p.m.

Colin puts his racquet bag and laptop onto the scanning belt.

His father is still there, arms folded across his chest, cheater glasses hooked into the neck of his fishing sweater. Chances are he will lose those glasses between now and when he eventually finds his car. But he will never lose that sweater.

Colin passes through the security gate and gathers his bag and laptop, puts on his shoes.

Turns to wave to his father.

He's gone.

10

COLIN

We're parked curbside in the handicapped zone, twenty feet from the baggage claim door, engine idling like a junkie in detox. Watching the flow of luggage-dragging travelers as they exit, hoping Ceo is among them soon. A silver-haired woman smoking a cigarette and leaning on a cane is giving us icy death glares. She starts wobbling toward a blue-uniformed guy in an orange vest who so far has been willing to ignore us.

"Looks like we're about to get busted," I say.

"Shit," Grahame says. "What the hell is taking so long?" He pulls out his phone. "I'm going to text him, find out what the fu—" and stops midsentence. A striking woman in a curve-hugging blue dress, midthirties, walks out the door towing a huge suitcase. "So there's our problem. He was hitting on that." A shuttle bus pulls up. The driver comes out, stows her bag, and they leave. Meanwhile Cane Lady has almost reached the guy in the vest.

Grahame says, "I vote we just leave his ass. We can hike to Cannabis Cove on our own."

A family of three exits, then twenty seconds later another female, alone. This one is high school age or maybe early college. Unlike the woman in the blue dress, she's wearing a loose long-sleeve shirt and comfortable shorts with big pockets. In Ceo's world, that would be one strike because where women's clothing is concerned, he elevates form over function. She's not the right height for him either, meaning she's tall. Ceo is a half inch short of six feet (although he can still dunk a basketball). He doesn't like his date to be taller than him if she's wearing heels, and he likes heels, the higher the better. She's probably pushing five eleven, so if she was his prom date, she'd have to wear flip-flops or go barefoot. Strike two. Her hair is black, which is good, but it doesn't quite reach her shoulders. Although Ceo has been known to go for girls with short hair, it isn't his preference. He says there's something about long hair down a naked back that really "cranks his dial." Call it strike two and a half because Ceo would say *hair grows*. I shake my head, realizing how sad it is that I evaluate every female I see relative to their score on Ceo's scale of attraction. But the biggest reason I'm noticing her at this moment isn't because she doesn't have a suitcase, or bag, or even a purse. She's wearing hiking boots. Who wears those on a plane?

Grahame says, "Look at doze legs, eh, mon. She's an athlete for sure. I'd geev her da tennis lessons for free, don't cha know."

She scans the traffic, then focuses directly on the Cherokee. For a second our eyes lock, and I get the distinct feeling that she was specifically looking for us. She taps out a text.

Ceo exits the door carrying a backpack, walks right up to her, and starts talking. She points to us. They go back and forth a couple times. Then Ceo moves closer. It's an intimate distance now. They have another conversation. She sticks her phone in his face. Then she looks at us again. Grahame just sits there, but his eyes narrow. I figure why not and raise my hand and wave while Grahame mutters, *Unfuckingreal,* and guns the engine. She sends another text. Ceo smiles. They start walking toward the car.

Grahame says, "Is he freaking serious?"

"Surprise," I say.

Cane Lady is talking to Vest Guy. He motions for us to move. Now.

Grahame gives the horn two quick blasts.

Ceo jogs to the back of the SUV, pops the lid, slings her pack on top of ours. He climbs in behind Grahame. She takes the seat behind me. Doors close.

Ceo says, "Guys, meet Ellie. Ellie, meet the guys."

All I can think about are those long legs all jammed up behind me. I scoot my seat so far forward my knees bump up against the dash.

Ceo laughs and says, "Q, she's tall. But she's not a freaking giraffe."

Cane Lady flips us the bird while Grahame pulls away from the curb asking, "Where to now, chief?"

Ceo yells, "To Yosemite and beyond!"

11

COLIN

C eo does most of the talking, telling us the story of how he and Ellie came to be. He said they met at acting camp, a fact that Ellie promptly disputed. She said it was a *theater arts and technology workshop*, not a camp. There were no tents, no bonfires, no mosquitoes or outhouses or dividing up into tribes and learning how to make soup from discarded snakeskins. She said one of her instructors had two Oscar nominations for cinematography. And Ceo learned how to channel his character's inner voice from Kevin Spacey's acting coach.

Ceo banged his head against the window and said, "Okay, okay, you win! It wasn't a camp."

But here's the thing about all that. I'd already heard too many stories from Ceo about this alleged "acting camp." Starting off with how much he didn't want to go but his agent said you do this or you'll never make the jump from stage to screen. So he grudgingly attended an intensive two-week workshop in Santa Cruz ($10,500, according to the website), then happily played the SoCal junior tournament circuit with Grahame for the rest of the summer. Meanwhile I was back in Vermont working seven to four at the fish hatchery. Ceo would text me a couple times a day, usually something desperate from his private ocean-view room on the Santa Cruz campus. He'd plead with me to rescue him from this unbearable torture. Then he'd share a studio head shot of a girl he just did a scene with who also happened to be a model who invariably wanted to "practice technique" with him later. I distinctly remember thinking at the time that if he's being tortured, then what do you call three months of squeezing roe out of the ass end of a rainbow trout?

What I don't remember during that time is anything about a girlfriend or potential girlfriend material. He never mentioned anyone that he had any interest in seeing beyond his "internment." As far as I know, he didn't stay in touch with any of the participants. So when Ellie climbed into the seat behind me and said she's going to open the window because it smells like man-feet in here, I was thinking what Grahame was probably thinking: this is some random girl Ceo met last week while standing in line at a taco truck, or buying shoes at the mall, or just performing the simple act of breathing with his shirt off. She will join the endless procession of heavenly bodies that pass through his gravitational field.

When he told us where he met her, I detected a disturbance in the field. When he said she's a genius with a camera, she can memorize an entire scene in five minutes and not miss a single line of dialogue, can add any five numbers in her head, and oh by the way, soccer fans (meaning me), *Sports Illustrated* ranks her among the top ten high school goalkeepers in the whole freaking country, Grahame and I shared a look of total bewilderment. We'd gone from a disturbance in the field to a massive disruption. Unlike his previous heavenly bodies, Ellie wasn't wearing any makeup. She wasn't the shortest person in this car. And she clearly stated when Grahame inanely asked her if she's a model, "No, I'm not, nor do I ever aspire to be one."

Consequently my head is spinning with this one inescapable conclusion: Ellie is the first girl, in the history of planet Ceo, where it might be argued that he put *function* ahead of *form*. But as I ponder the entire Ellie package, it would be a very close call.

During Ceo's mostly true retelling of the events at Santa Cruz, we watched with growing concern as a thin wisp of black on the horizon refused to go away. Now, with rolling hills and farmland yielding to the pine-crusted shoulders of almost-mountains, the wisp has transformed into a wind-bent smudge, staining an otherwise blue sky the color of LA smog. We can't find anything on the web about a fire in Yosemite, so maybe it's not an issue. This is California in the fall, Ceo says, yawning. There's always a fire somewhere to put out. Then he asks Ellie if she'd like to know some interesting facts about the other occupants in the car.

He tells her Grahame is from Las Vegas, where his father runs security for three casinos, that he transferred into CGA a year ago and went undefeated in the league at number one singles, then proceeded to win state without dropping a set. Another interesting fact is Grahame's brother plays outside linebacker for the Patriots and has two Super Bowl rings. And in two weeks Grahame is taking the ASVAB because he wants to be an Army Ranger. It strikes me while Ceo talks that he sounds like a game-show host introducing today's contestants.

Ellie asks Grahame, Why the Rangers and not the SEALs? Grahame says he sinks like a sack of stones and would never pass the water test. Ceo asks Ellie to please, *please* don't *ever* tell Grahame that you like Bob Marley or any of this steel-drum Caribbean shit we've been listening to for the past million miles. She asks, Why, what's wrong with it? He says, Because Grahame starts talking like a drunken Jamaican pimp from Fargo, and you won't be able to understand a freaking word out of his mouth. Ellie says she likes reggae, especially before it went rap, and listens to Beenie Man when she's going through pregame drills. Grahame lights up for the first time since we left the airport. He says, Ooh ooh, me tinks you be too good a woo-mon ta be datin' da model-mon, don't cha know. Ellie says, Ya be speakin' da truth, meester Ranger mon. Ceo groans, says, Oh shit, there's no stopping him now. Then he leans forward between the seats, saying, And now for my good friend from—

12

ELLIE

"**D**on't tell me," she says. "Let me guess."

"Okay," Ceo says. "Tell us what you know about the mysterious Q."

"Colin is from Vermont. He plays soccer and likes movies. And he's a John Cusack fan."

Silence under the music. She waits. Grahame is nodding. Maybe because he's impressed. Maybe it's just the music. He's the hardest of the three to figure out. Ceo's smiling, his eyes on Colin.

Colin says, "How did you know I'm from Vermont?"

Ellie says, "Why do you think?"

"My syrupy accent?"

"Nope. It was on the school website. You were eight and two last year, plus one forfeit on the last match of the season. What happened there? Did you get hurt?"

Ceo looks at her, shakes his head.

After a long beat Colin says, "How did you know I like movies?"

She makes a mental note that he skipped the forfeit question.

"Someone in this car is reading *Good Will Hunting*. You have to like movies to read screenplays. I know it isn't Ceo because he doesn't read. Not even my texts."

Ceo shoots her a puzzled *where did that come from* look. He smiles, hoping for one in return. She leaves him hanging.

Grahame says, "How do you know I'm not reading that screenplay?"

"There's a bookmark in the pivotal scene where Sean tells Professor Lambeau that Will counted down the seconds in his head. The bookmark is from the Flying Pig Bookstore with an address in Shelburne, Vermont. Unless you're from Vermont, which I doubt because you're driving and this car has Nevada plates, that makes Colin the screenplay-reading movie fan from Vermont."

"Why is that scene pivotal?" Colin asks.

"It's why Sean accepts the challenge," she says. "Without that scene, you don't have a movie." Ellie waits for the next question. Hopes it's the one she wants to hear.

Colin says, "How did you know I'm a Cusack fan?"

There it is. She smiles at the back of his seat, wishes she could see his face.

Ellie says, "To hang on to sanity too tight is insane."

She hears a laugh, then, "You saw my note on the back page."

"*Pushing Tin*, 1999, with Billy Bob Thornton and Cate Blanchett."

"That was a great line in a not-so-great movie."

"Definitely not in his top ten," she says, not telling him she posted that exact quote on her Facebook page two weeks ago. Then she asks, "How about this one: *I'm a paranoid schizophrenic. I'm my own entourage.*"

Colin says, "You're going to have to dig deeper than that. *America's Sweethearts* with Billy Crystal and Julia Roberts."

Ceo says, "I think that guy is overrated. Too many words. He needs to just shut up and act."

Colin says, "Like Jason Statham?"

"Exactly. Let his fists do the talking."

They pass a Welcome to Oakhurst sign, and Grahame slows down to match the flow of traffic. Ellie asks him to make a quick stop at the next convenience store, which she's relieved to see a minute later. As they're pulling into the lot, Ceo says to Ellie, "You didn't tell us how you knew Q played soccer."

"That's a simple one. You told me."

"I did?"

"You said he played midfield but had to stop because of tennis."

"I said all that?"

She nods.

"When?"

Showing him a smile this time, she says, "At the beach."

It's Poker Saturday, and as usual Colin is the first to fold.

Sometimes he delays the inevitable by dipping into his emergency ATM, which is the envelope his father gave him at the Burlington airport. This is where he keeps whatever is left over from stringing the occasional racquet. He keeps the envelope in The Collected Poems of Robert Frost *next to his bed, marking the "Road Not Taken" page to remind him why he's here and not back in Vermont. His father told* *him he should always have a fifty for emergencies without really defining the term. His friends at the table tell him this is an emergency no doubt because he doesn't want to be the snack and beverage bitch yet again, right? Colin briefly considers their logic, and finds it full of flaws. September was an expensive month, with two textbooks that weren't included in his "scholarship," plus his uniform deposit, which Coach couldn't get waived this year due to cutbacks in athletics, so there's an unexpected $150 hit to his monthly budget. But all that is, as his father would say, matters of substantial inconsequence, compared to the post-challenge-match financial crater he's staring at now. He resigns himself to filling the snack bowl and fetching Mountain Dews, which, per their agreement, he must also open because that is the price you pay for folding first.*

Rhody is next up on the poker food chain, then it's down to the inevitable Ceo vs. Grahame bluff-fest, which Ceo with the deeper pockets usually wins but not tonight. As the smiling Grahame rakes in the mound of quarters with a few singles mixed in, saying, Gentlemen I believe this is the biggest pot of the night, Ceo announces that speaking of pot, I have a proposition for the group. But first I must share the tale behind it.

He tells them about a drug-smuggling plane that crashed in a remote mountain lake in Yosemite back in the seventies. The rock climbers got to it before the rangers did, scoring a lifetime's worth of prime Colombian weed and spiking the local economy with a flood of money and flashy cars. The plane and the weed are long gone, but the legend lives on. Movies have been made on the subject.

Grahame shuffles the cards and says, Mon, dat's a fine story, don't cha know, so what be da proposition?

Ceo asks Grahame to switch the music to Game of Thrones. *With that symphony of drama pulsing in the background, he says a tale this epic deserves a pilgrimage up to that lake.*

Rhody asks him to define pilgrimage.

Ceo says, A ten-mile hike one way.

Grahame asks, Does this mean real camping with sleeping bags 'n' shit?

Ceo says, Yes, especially the shit.

Ceo and Grahame share a smile, suggesting there might be more than just woodsmoke rising up from their campfire. That adds potential dimensions to this trip that Colin would rather weren't there. His head starts swirling with the repercussions of Ceo's unfolding plan.

Rhody asks, How will this pilgrimage happen, seeing as we can't get away for a weekend unless it's approved by the faculty?

Ceo reminds them that Coach is going back east for a wedding the third weekend of October, and there happens to be a tournament in San Diego that very same weekend.

Colin says, We still need Coach to sign off.

Ceo says, We'll use the note from last year. Rhody can change the dates and location, then hack into the server and upload it. Right, Rhody?

Not a problem, Rhody says.

Colin asks what if he checks the results online.

Ceo says, He'll be in freaking Boston getting wrecked at a wedding. It's preseason and not a sanctioned tournament.

He won't give a shit. Rhody says, I could build a bogus website with bogus results.

Ceo says, There you go. Problem solved. It's time to ante up, my friends. Are we pilgrims or not?

Grahame says, Will the pilgrims be just us four guys?

Ceo says, Yes, absolutely. Just us four.

Grahame says, Solemn poker vow?

Solemn poker vow, Ceo confirms.

After a beat Grahame says, If it's just us, then I'm in.

Rhody says, Sure, if I don't have any tests.

All eyes turn to Colin.

He says, We don't have any gear.

Ceo shrugs. I'll get what I have from home. Craigslist will take care of the rest.

Colin thinks about costs. About the work he'll be missing, the studying that won't get done, the physics test he won't be ready for when he gets back. Lying to Coach. But all that is dwarfed by the fact that he's still reeling from what Ceo did at the match and the profound impact it will have on his future at CGA. Coach said Mad Maxine has already contacted him about his student-athlete endowment status for the spring semester. The fact that it's his senior year has no bearing on the outcome. Rules are rules. His mother cried when he told her that he dropped out of the top two and was going to lose the scholarship. She offered to sell the tractor, take out a loan, whatever he needed to stay. He said no, he'd find a way to make it work, although folding towels for ten bucks an hour wouldn't cut it. Meanwhile Ceo sits across from him with a hopeful smile, acting like their friendship is back to the status quo. Like he's moved on, and so should Colin. But he's not staring at thirty grand in debt and the possibility of transferring back to Vermont. Doubting Ceo will get the deeper meaning, Colin says, Guys, I can't afford this.

Grahame says, Dat's da bool-sheet, mon.

Ceo says, C'mon, Q! We'll divide the expenses four ways. You have to *eat anyway, so that expense cancels out. All we're really talking about is the gas. Fifty bucks per person, tops. You must have that squirreled away in your little envelope.*

Grahame and Rhody nod at the logic.

Colin feels his resolve withering under the heat of their expectant smiles. He can't give up the cash destined for textbooks, but there is a fifty-dollar gift certificate to Foot Locker his father gave him at the airport. Grahame could buy that with tonight's haul. He looks at his tennis sneakers by the door. Gaping holes in both. With duct tape and more glue they can last another month.

Ceo says, C'mon, Q, fifty bucks is nothing for a memory that will last a lifetime.

Colin still hesitates.

Eyes boring into his, Ceo says, Hey, you and I, man. We need this.

And the dorm room fills with the sound of Colin's wall of resistance cracking, then falling to the floor. He decides he needs to go on this trip more than he needs to be left behind.

The Ceo Effect strikes again.

Colin says okay, okay. I'm in. But I'm not getting high, so don't even ask.

Ceo beams, raises his can of Dew, and toasts to the pilgrims four.

Grahame asks, What's the name of our epic destination?

Ceo says, Lower Merced Pass Lake. But in honor of Grahame's future in the army, let's call it Operation Cannabis Cove.

13

COLIN

We're parked nose-in at a Chevron in Oakhurst, facing the store windows, where Miller Lite is on sale by the case for $12.99 and the Powerball is at $256 million. Ellie headed straight for the back, disappeared through a door, and that's where she's been for at least two songs. She seemed in a hurry. Ceo is searching his phone for news about the fire, and Grahame has been silent since we parked. With him you never know if that is a good thing or not. I'm still spinning from Ellie's knowledge of John Cusack and her spot-on analysis of my favorite scene from *Good Will Hunting* when Grahame asks Ceo if Ellie really is one of the best goalies in the country.

Ceo says, "She got the state record for consecutive shutouts—in her *sophomore year.*"

Grahame says, "Maybe she has a really good defense backing her up."

"Dude, she's on the U-18 national team. She played in Barcelona in June and had a shutout against freaking Brazil."

"So she's really good."

"Yeah. Like really freaking good."

"What about you?"

"What about me?"

Grinning back at Ceo, he says, "Have you scored on her yet?"

After a beat, "No comment."

"You know what I think?"

"No comment."

"I think she's got another shutout going."

"Still no comment."

Grahame smiles at me. He's just getting warmed up.

"So da question, sports fans," he says, "ees will da Ceo-mon end da shutout?"

Ceo says nothing. But I hear him breathing. Like a bull in a ring.

Grahame looks at me, still with that smile. His teeth are huge, matching the rest of him. He says, "Q. Wanna bet Ceo tries to slip one into the goal tonight?"

Ceo slams his fist into the back of Grahame's seat. The impact is so hard it snaps Grahame's body forward. Grahame laughs.

Ceo says with his voice controlled but working hard to keep it that way, "What we do or don't do is none of your business."

Grahame says, "Here's an update, chief: it's *totally* my business."

The only good thing about this situation is that they're separated by a seat. Even though Grahame has Ceo by three inches and forty pounds, Ceo won't back down. I say, "You both need to shut up and listen to Bob Freaking Marley," and crank the volume way up. The Cherokee starts vibrating.

Ceo leans forward between the seats and shouts, "Dude, what's your fucking problem? She likes your dumb-ass reefer music."

Grahame shouts back, "You know what my problem is?"

"What? That she'd kick your ass in soccer?"

"My problem is you brought a chew toy on this trip."

"Why is that your problem?"

"You said it was guys only."

I turn down the music. If they're just going to shout, why bother? I glance at the store window, looking for signs of Ellie. She's two people back in the checkout line, phone out and texting. I say, "Let's wrap this up. We're all here to go camping. Commune with nature. Find our inner selves. Focus on that."

Ceo says, "Works for me. If Mister Chew Toy is done being an ass."

Grahame says over his shoulder, "Have you told her about Cannabis Cove?"

"Not yet."

"Why not?"

"Because I haven't."

"Does she even get high?"

"I don't know. I'm guessing probably not."

"She's your girlfriend and you don't even know if she smokes?"

Ceo doesn't answer. Ellie is at the register paying with cash.

Grahame says, "Give me Rhody's share of the weed and I'm good."

I say, "Here she comes. Time to put away your knives."

Ceo says to Grahame, "I have an update to your update. There is no weed."

"No weed?" Grahame hisses. "What the *fuck*?" This is news for me too. Good news, actually, but not for Grahame. For him it's like he's five years old and his father just told him Christmas is canceled because Santa got drunk with the elves and forgot where he parked his sleigh.

It's Ceo's turn to smile. "Dude, floor tickets for the Lakers are not cheap."

14

ELLIE

Ellie stands in line for the register, grateful to be out of what could be the rankest bathroom of all time. She's waiting behind a man in a Harley jacket with a beard the size of a horse's tail, pondering the choice she made a minute ago and is already regretting. A thumping bass beat out the window distracts her. She turns, along with all the other heads in line, to find the source. She's pretty sure it's from the Cherokee because that same beat has been playing in her head ever since they left the airport. Ceo is leaning forward between the seats. He appears to be shouting, probably trying to be heard over the music. Grahame smiles at whatever Ceo is saying. Colin is turned, facing Ceo. All she sees of him is the back of his head.

Her phone dings.

NADIA

Where are u?

ELLIE

> A Chevron in Oakhurst.

NADIA

> Hows Mr. Abs?

> I met the friends.

> And?

> All guys.

The music stops thumping, and the line shuffles forward. Now it's Beard Man buying six Powerballs and a tin of Skoal. She wonders if she should tell Nadia about her decision.

> Yikes! Are you ok?

> One likes JC and plays soccer.

NADIA

> Your twin lives!
>
> Does he know Newton?

ELLIE

> TBD. Gotta go.

It's her turn to pay. She puts her purchases in a neat little pile on the counter: an emergency two-pack of Kotex lights and dental floss. And a box of condoms. She was walking past the display, stopped, thought for a moment, then did what she never does—made a spontaneous decision of significant import without weighing all the variables, X, Y, and C for Ceo. Never having bought this product before, she grabbed the box with the most wilderness-sounding name, *Trojan Bareskin*, and went with that. She thought about consulting with the ultimate resource, Nadia, but chose to not go there. She's pretty sure Beard Man would have been happy to share his thoughts on the subject as well.

The clerk, a kind gray-haired man with weary eyes, rings up the Kotex, then the floss. Just as he's reaching for the condoms, Ellie tucks the box behind a display of Hostess cupcakes. She replaces them with a box of cinnamon Tic Tacs.

The old guy says, "They don't do the same thing."

Ellie says, "I know."

He looks out the window at the Cherokee, then blinks his weary eyes at her.

"You sure?"

"Yes."

The woman behind her coughs.

"That'll be five seventy-five," the old guy says, and gives her change for a ten. "Would you like a bag for these items?" he asks.

"No, thanks," Ellie says, "I have pockets." She exits the store and heads for the Cherokee, which is roaring to life, feeling those weary eyes on her back all the way to the car.

15
COLIN

Ellie opens the door and climbs in. We smile at her like monkeys in a banana tree. If she bought something, I don't see it.

Grahame says as he's backing out, "Ellie, did you buy any gum?"

"No. Why?"

"Ceo needs a chew toy."

"What does that mean?" Her seat belt clips in.

"Just ignore him," Ceo says. "Were you successful?"

"I was." She shows him a pack of Tic Tacs. "Want one? They're cinnamon."

16

COLIN

After the Oakhurst stop the conversations align geographically, with Ceo and Ellie talking quietly in the back. I hear her laugh a couple of times, so Ceo must be working his magic. The smell of cinnamon Tic Tacs fills the air. Meanwhile I'm up front drilling Grahame with questions from the ASVAB practice site. That ends abruptly when his Samsung drops the signal and my crappy phone is not an option, with my battery indicator flashing red.

Every few minutes Ceo emerges from his conversation with Ellie to ask Grahame to please oh please stop playing Bob Freaking Marley. He seriously doesn't want that music in his head when he's hiking up the trail. Grahame finally complies by punching up the sound track to *Game of Thrones*. It's an improvement, but not without a cost. Grahame descends into silent mode. Since I don't want to eavesdrop on the backseat dialogue, I watch big, ancient trees flash past my window and contemplate the recent chain of events that led to me occupying this seat on this day. I start at last Saturday's poker game and work my way back from there. It was this very same song that was playing in the background when Ceo pitched the pilgrimage to Cannabis Cove.

I work my way farther back, landing on the day I arrived in LA from Vermont, blinking at the palm trees and worried about the scope of my decision. That transferring out of my high school and away from my friends to a school for the über rich that would put my family into eons of debt, even with my scholarship, was a burden so heavy I was surprised the plane was able to take off. Coach sent Ceo to pick me up, and we've been oddly paired friends ever since. So when Ceo whispered those words at the poker game, the only real option I had was to swallow what was left of my pride and agree. Yeah, I pretty much caved.

So here I am, in this seat, watching the scenery flow by.

Then Grahame, out of the blue, asks me what I'm doing for Thanksgiving.

I tell him, "I'm not sure. Why?"

"We always have a huge dinner at our house. Dad has one of the casinos cater it, Mom hires a pastry chef to make these amazing pies. There's always way more food than mouths to eat it. And this year my brother has a game against Denver. Dad had a theater built in the basement just to watch him play."

"Sounds like a good time," I say, not even able to imagine what a Thanksgiving like that would look like.

"So, anyway, what I'm thinking is if you're not doing anything, I can ditch my plane ticket and we can drive to Vegas in the Cherokee."

I notice that the conversation in the backseat has stopped. I wonder if that's because Ceo made me the same offer, but at their house in Big Sur. I said no because I was planning on going home to Vermont to have dinner with my mom. It would be her first Thanksgiving without Dad, and I didn't want her to eat alone. But my financial situation has changed now that my scholarship is a smoldering ash heap. I canceled my flight, took the partial refund, and hoped to pick up hours at work while I still have a job.

Knowing that Ceo is listening, I say, "Sounds like fun. But I need to be back for work on Sunday."

Grahame says, "Cool. I'll tell Mom we'll have a Vermonter coming for dinner. She'll freak."

More silence from the backseat. We pass a sign announcing that Yosemite is six miles away.

Ellie breaks the backseat silence by saying she has a question for me, if that's okay.

I say, "Sure. What is it?"

"I'm wondering why, out of all the great quotes by John Cusack, you picked that specific quote?"

Ceo says, "Shit. You mean there's more than one?"

I look over my shoulder at her, needing to know if she's serious or if she's just joking around, in which case I will avoid the truth and make something up. She's leaning forward against her seat belt, eyes straight ahead and focused. She has the kind of eyes that know which way a foot is going to kick a ball before the laces hit the leather. I have this feeling that if my answer is remotely untrue, she will call me out on it, or worse, apologize for asking.

I say, "It's a compass quote."

Ceo says, "Remind me again. What was this amazing Cusack quote?"

Ellie says, "'To hang on to sanity too long is insane.' Here, suck on this." I hear the Tic Tacs shake. Then she grabs the back of my seat. "So tell me, Colin. What is a compass quote?"

"You sure you want to hear this?"

"Absolutely."

"All right. My father collected old compasses. He had over two hundred of them, some dating back to the days of Ethan Allen and Fort Ticonderoga. He kept them in a felt-lined wooden box in the basement. In that same box was a folded sheet of paper with twenty handwritten quotes by people ranging from Ben Franklin to Maya Angelou and Steve Jobs. I asked him why he kept those quotes in the box with the compasses. He said good quotes and good compasses do the same thing. They help you find your way through the woods when you're lost. He called them compass quotes. So back to your question, that Cusack quote helped me find my way."

"To California?" she asked.

"No," I say, and take a breath. "It helped me navigate through the residues of life." I look over my shoulder and catch her nodding.

She says, "The residues of life. I like that."

"It comes straight from my dad."

She leans back in her seat and smiles.

Grahame rounds a corner. There it is, the gate with a big sign welcoming us to Yosemite National Park. He drives up to the line three cars deep.

While Grahame creeps forward, Ceo says, "Ellie. I have a question for you."

"Go on."

"What are your thoughts on Smurfs?"

It takes her thirty seconds to respond, which is twenty-nine seconds longer than the question deserves. I glance in the rearview to see what's going on. Ceo is focused on her. She's looking out the window.

"Well?" Ceo says as Grahame pulls up to the gate.

"They're not completely harmless," Ellie says. "But they're harmless enough."

17
ELLIE

Ellie heard Nadia's text come in when Colin was talking about his father.

She resisted checking then because his answer was more than she expected. He talked about his father in the past tense; she heard the notes of sadness around the edges and wanted to know more about the residues of his life. She liked the vision of the right words as an unwavering needle pointing the way and wondered what her compass quotes would be. Before that thought crystalized, Ceo asked her the Smurf question.

Ellie remembered looking at the tattooed barista, believing that Newton's first law was the reason behind it all. Behind her willingness to tear open the neatly wrapped package of her life. Her willingness to tell lies to her parents, friends, and teammates. All that and more so she could set this object in motion. She told Ceo that Smurfs aren't harmless but *they're harmless enough*. He smiled the way he smiled at her at the beach, then leaned across the seat, tucked a strand of hair behind an ear, and kissed her on the cheek.

*   *   *

The car ahead of them pulls a U-ie on the other side of the booth and leaves. A frowning kid in the backseat waves to her as they pass. It looked like the two adults in the front seat were fighting. Grahame drives up to the booth, lowers his window, and asks the uniformed woman inside, "So where's the fire, ma'am?"

"In a box canyon six miles southeast of here."

"How bad is it?"

"Eighty percent contained. If the wind doesn't pick up ahead of the storm, it will be out by tomorrow afternoon. But it's going to be smoky in some areas for the rest of the weekend. Where are you headed?"

"Lower Merced Pass Lake."

She shakes her head. "Sorry. Access to that trail is limited to emergency personnel only."

Ceo lowers his window. "What's it like in the valley?"

"About like it is here. Not a good day for pictures. And we don't recommend going if you have respiratory issues."

Ceo asks Ellie, "Do you have any respiratory issues?"

"None," she says. "But my eyes are allergic to smoke."

Ceo asks the woman, "What's it like above the rim?"

"All clear on the north side."

Grahame says, "So what's the plan, chief?"

Ceo says, "I vote we head into the valley and figure it out from there."

An engine rumbles behind them. Ellie looks out the rear window. Two men on Harleys are at the front of a very long line.

The woman says, "Sir, you need pay the entry fee or pull forward and turn around."

Grahame says to Ceo, "What about the pilgrimage?"

Ceo shrugs. "No cannabis, no cove."

Ellie thinks, Cannabis?

Grahame looks at Colin. "Am I dah only one here dat smells dah fookin' bool-sheet?"

Ceo says, "Dude, what's it going to take for you to stop talking like that?"

Grahame says, "Eets dah way ah talk when you be deeshin' dah bool-sheet."

"Maybe this will work," Ceo says.

Ellie watches him pull out his wallet, remove a thick wad of cash, and peel off a hundred-dollar bill. He rips the hundred in half, slaps one half on the armrest between Grahame and Colin. "You'll get the other half if you don't talk like a toothless Jamaican mobster pimp for the rest of the trip. Does that work for you?"

Grahame pockets the shredded bill, winks at Ellie in the mirror. "*Sí, señor.*"

A quarter mile from the Wawona Tunnel she remembers to check her phone. It's a good thing she didn't wait a minute longer because her reception is nearly gone. There are two texts, not one. The first is from Nadia. It's a screenshot of Ellie's Instagram, where she posted the fake picture of Ellie with Jenny, the fake admissions representative she met on her fake visit to Pepperdine. The picture has seventeen likes, two of them being from her sister and her mother.

The second text is from her mother.

JANICE BOYER

Dad set up a lunch date on Sat. with Dr. Halliday. His office number is 310-555-4426. He's expecting your call. Have fun in Malibu. We're all so proud of you!

THE TRAIL

Colin is waiting outside the terminal, not sure who or what to look for. The text said someone was on the way. He blinks at the sunlight filtering down through the exhaust of circling shuttle buses and taxis. Not too far away are palm trees, their leaves covered with dust, but the green looks good against the blue sky.

A red two-seater Mercedes convertible pulls up to the curb, and the trunk lid opens.

The driver gets out, shouts over the traffic, Are you Colin?

Yes.

Load your shit and let's go.

Colin tosses his racquet bag and carry-on into the trunk and climbs into the front seat. Smells leather and coconut oil. And . . . perfume? The music is something that sounds like Pearl Jam but isn't.

The guy screeches away from the curb into the flow of traffic. He turns to Colin, reaches out his right hand for a shake, and says, I'm Ceo.

I'm Colin.

Ceo tells him Coach couldn't make it, so it's my job to entertain you till practice tomorrow.

Colin says, Thanks, then to keep things going he adds, this is my first time in a Mercedes.

Ceo says, This is my first time with a Vermonter.

Colin tells him Vermonters don't get out much. They're basically hobbits.

Ceo says, Dude, I'll never go to your state.

Why? Colin asks.

I hate maple. The taste, the smell, the fucking word. Brrrruugh. So I won't go to Vermont because of all those freaking maple trees.

Colin says, Good to know, thinking about all the maple treats his mother insisted he bring for gifts.

Ceo puts on aviator sunglasses. Dark, like the leather seats. They reflect the sky.

He says, Do you have Frisbees in Vermont, Colin?

We've had the technology for two years. They're starting to catch on.

Ceo regards him for a beat with those glasses. Says, Two years is no excuse. You better have skills because if you suck, then you might as well go home.

He grins wide, says, We're going to the beach, and pushes a button on the dash. The top opens up and folds behind them. Ceo's hair floats across his tanned face like a mane of yellow in the wind.

Colin thinks he's never seen anything quite like it.

Except in magazines and movies.

18
COLIN

Ceo insists we stop on the other side of the Wawona Tunnel. He says if Q's going to pop his Yosemite cherry, that's the proper place to do it. I've seen pictures of Yosemite from Inspiration Point, so I know what to expect. But my eyes still water when we exit the tunnel and park at the overlook. It's like we traveled back in time to this vast, scooped-out valley complete with thousand-foot waterfalls and everything all green and gold and so screamingly ancient I find myself expecting to see the heads of long-necked dinosaurs grazing on treetops.

But all is not right in the valley.

Massive granite walls rise up from a translucent yellow-brown smoky haze. The air has the disturbing scent of charred wood with an occasional ash flake floating down like the one I just blew off my hand. Unlike the camera-toting folks from the four charter buses idling nearby, I don't bother taking pictures. No sense wasting the little juice my phone has left.

Ceo asks a woman to take a picture of the four of us. We line up, Grahame, me, Ceo, Ellie, backs to the expanse, and she takes the shot. Then Ceo asks her to take one more and changes places with Ellie. That move strikes me as odd, and I'm sure my confusion shows when she counts to three and snaps the second pic.

On the way back to the car Ceo walks with Grahame, talking about something I can't hear. He points up to the valley rim; Grahame nods and laughs. Fifty yards from the car Ellie tells me she feels like she's seen me before. That I'm familiar and she can't line up my face with the where and the when, which is unusual for her, and that's been bugging her since the airport.

I could go with the truth and nearly do. But at the last second it ducks into the shadows, and I'm left with my old friend, the fish. I say you probably saw my picture. It was on page four in the C section of the *Burlington Free Press*. When I was eleven I just missed the state walleye ice-fishing record by a quarter ounce.

She says, "To be so young and so close. What's it like being a quarter ounce from number one?"

I say, "Five years of hypnotherapy and I still ask myself every day how different would my life be if that fish hadn't skipped breakfast before it bit my yellow-tailed jig."

I catch her studying me with those miss-nothing eyes just before we get into the Cherokee. I say, "There's a different story that doesn't involve a fish."

She smiles. "I'd like to hear that story."

All I can see from there to the valley floor are those eyes and the smile below it.

Since the pilgrimage to Cannabis Cove went up in literal flames, we need a plan B. Our first stop is the visitor center, where Ceo buys *Best Backpacking Trips and Trails of Yosemite and the Central Sierra*. We assemble outside in the smoky air to discuss our options.

Ellie says, "Whatever you decide is fine with me. I need to take care of something," and she walks back into the visitor center.

Grahame, watching her go, says, "Is she using the restroom again?"

"Why?" Ceo says. "Is there a limit?"

"Just making an observation."

"About what?"

"It seems like a lot to me."

"Meaning what exactly?"

"Nothing. Forget I mentioned it."

"I'll just add it to the crazy-shit-you-say list."

Ceo starts rattling off trail descriptions and their highlights. I know I should be listening, but it really doesn't matter to me which trail we take out of the smoke. It's going to be a thigh-busting grind no matter what. I can deal with that. What I'm having problems with is what I heard when Ceo leaned over in the Cherokee. I'm pretty sure he kissed her, and it's really crazy how this is spinning me because (a) they weren't, like, *making out*, and (b) she's with him and that's

How. It. Is.

I've been friends with Ceo long enough to know when girls are present, he is the sun and I am the shadow. But I keep thinking about Ellie's John Cusack question (I've never told anyone about the compass quotes), and the smile she gave me at the overlook. For a moment, one blindingly ridiculous moment, I knew what it felt like to be the sun. Now the thought of her spending two nights in a tent with a confessed Cusack hater—while I'm rubbing shoulders with Grahame—is a tough pill to swallow. But swallow I must because Ceo says he's found it, the ultimate freaking trail.

He reads us the description and highlights, making sure to emphasize 2,600 feet of elevation gain in 1.5 miles, 108 switchbacks, and the fact that the Snow Creek Trail is widely considered the toughest trail out of the valley.

When he's done, he looks at Grahame and says, "Well?"

Grahame nods. "That could work."

They share a smile. Bump fists.

"What could work?" I ask.

"LMS," Ceo says, "to the freaking top."

On Tuesdays and Thursdays Coach has us run bleachers. It's the most dreaded drill we do. Ceo would always beat everyone—until Grahame transferred in last year. They turned it into a race called Last Man Standing, or LMS. The winner laps the stadium twice, or someone collapses, whichever comes first. Vomiting is usually involved, along with some kind of demeaning wager designed to humiliate the loser. Coach outlawed LMS after Rhody fell down a flight of stairs, resulting in a separated collarbone and an ambulance ride to the hospital.

I look up at the valley rim. The distance is staggeringly vertical. I can't imagine hiking it, let alone running it. "When did you come up with this insanity?" I ask.

"At the overlook," Ceo says. "I suggested it to Grahame, and he said sure, if I found the right trail. One hundred eight switchbacks in one point five miles sounds right to me."

"With packs on?"

"Even better."

Ellie returns in time to see them bumping fists again.

"What did I miss?" she asks.

There's something odd about her voice, a slight shake to it that wasn't there before.

"These guys are going to race to the top," I say.

"In this air?" Her voice is back to its steady self.

"No worse than running on Wilshire in the summer," Grahame says.

Ceo says to us, "You two are welcome to join."

"I'll pass," I say. "Someone needs to notify your next of kin."

Ellie rolls her eyes, like *let the stupid begin*.

Ceo says to Grahame, "So what's on the table?"

"It needs to be something good. Something special. A prize, you know"—Grahame looks straight at Ellie with a thin smile—"*worthy of the challenge*."

She doesn't flinch or turn away. For a sickening beat I think he's going to put her on the table.

Grahame says with his eyes still locked on hers, "Do you know CPR?"

"Yes."

"Good. When this is done, your man's gonna need chest compressions and mouth-to-mouth."

"He's not *my* man," Ellie says evenly. "*My* implies possession, and that was abolished in 1865."

Grahame considers her point. "Okay, whatever that means." Then to Ceo, "How about a Double-B for a week?"

"Make it two weeks and you have a deal."

Ceo offers a hand to Grahame.

They shake, grinning like hounds at a bunny hunt.

As we climb into the Cherokee I'm thinking about my dad and all those fish that found their way into his net. He said the secret isn't in the bait, it's in the presentation.

Poor Grahame.

He never felt the hook.

19

ELLIE

"I'd like to speak with Dr. Halliday."

"I'll see if he's in. Please hold."

Ellie listens to Vivaldi on the phone. Wishes something less cheerful were on, something more closely aligned with what she's about to do. She mentally rehearses what she's going to say while watching a little girl spin the postcard rack next to a woman wondering which stuffed animal is worth forty-five dollars, beaver or bear.

"Dr. Halliday speaking."

Ellie winces. She was hoping for voice mail. Oh well.

"Hi, Dr. Halliday. This is Ellie Boyer—"

"Oh, hi, Ellie! So nice to hear from you. I've been looking forward to our lunch. There's a new place in Temescal Canyon I'd like to try. You're not a vegetarian, are you?"

"No. I'm a flesh eater. But I need to—"

"Just a second. My travel agent is calling. Hold on."

Back to Vivaldi. Music to lie to, she thinks.

"Hi, Ellie. Sorry about that. I'm leaving for Brussels on Monday, and there's a hitch in my accommodations at that end. So where were we? Lunch. But first, how's your dad?"

"He's fine."

"Has he cured cancer yet?"

"No. But he gets closer every day."

"And Janice? The last time I saw her was at Pete's wedding. Your mom is an excellent dancer. Are you as good as her?"

"Yes she is, and no I'm not."

Polite laughter on the other end.

"So? How are you enjoying our campus?"

She looks outside. Evergreens and soaring cliffs. "It's beautiful. I love it here."

"Have you seen the soccer fields yet?"

"No. But that's a must for sure. Speaking of tomorrow, I'm afraid I can't make our lunch date."

A disappointed sigh at the other end. "I'm sorry to hear that. Hang on." She hears a keyboard clicking. "Luckily it looks like my afternoon tomorrow is wide open. We could switch our lunch to an early dinner if that works better for you."

"No. They have me on a pretty tight schedule."

"What do they have you doing?"

"Actually," she says, searching for something that is at least partly true, "I'm going on a hike."

"I didn't know hikes were part of the recruitment process."

"It was a special request on my part."

"Well, that shows how much we want you here."

"I guess."

"Where will you be hiking?"

"A park, but she didn't tell me which one."

"Probably Malibu Creek, or maybe Topanga Canyon."

"All I know is I'm supposed to bring sunscreen and a hat. Lunch will be provided."

"Who's taking you? I'd like to personally thank him or her for treating you so well."

"Jessie. I don't remember her last name. She's a student. From Texas."

Hears writing at the other end. "Is that Jessie with an *i* or a *y*?"

"An *ie*, I think." *Shit!*

"Well, looks like you have a perfect day. Hopefully, the weather up north won't make its way down here. Carl may have to cancel his tee time."

"He stopped playing golf because of his back. But that's another story. I'm sorry, but I have to go. My new friends are waiting."

"Okay, then. A rain check?"

"Yes. Absolutely."

"I hope you know that I was thrilled when your dad told me you were considering Pepperdine. We would love to have you. And, oh, before you go. I told Coach Hazeltine you were coming. He didn't know anything about your visit, but he'd love the opportunity to tell you about his program. Can you fit him in?"

"I'll try. Have fun in Brussels."

"I will. Enjoy your hike."

"It should be fun."

"Go Waves!"

"Go Waves."

She pockets her phone. Takes three deep breaths, refocuses on the mom at the register handing the bear to her daughter, who obviously wanted the beaver. Ellie walks outside, wondering how she'll ever listen to Vivaldi again without feeling sick.

20

COLIN

Grahame is worried the Cherokee will be towed, so he parks it in a far corner of the lot under a tree next to a Dumpster. Ceo says it's okay to leave it here through the weekend, but Grahame doesn't trust him or the guidebook. According to that same guidebook, this is where we pick up the Curry Village shuttle bus that takes us to the Mirror Lake Trail, and a mile past that, the Snow Creek Trail, where we start heading up out of the smoke via the 108 switchbacks from hell.

We talked in the car about picking up some snacks at the Village Store, but Ceo is obsessed with getting on the trail, and he and Grahame can't stop talking about their LMS race. We haul our packs out of the Cherokee and do the final adjustments. Ellie, Grahame, and I have old-school external packs with our sleeping bags strapped underneath or on top. The pack I'm using belongs to Ceo's sister and is a little small for my six-one frame. I wind up leaving a hoodie sweatshirt and an extra pair of warm-up pants behind because they just won't fit. That doesn't hurt as much as the discovery that I forgot my foam sleeping pad. Ceo offers to buy one, but I know that will take time that we can't afford. I say I can sleep on pine needles for two nights.

Ceo has a Mountain Hardwear pack with no visible frame. It's ultralight, ninja black with red straps and looks like something out of *Climbing* magazine. It matches his Mountain Hardwear pants and fleece hat and the down jacket I saw him stuffing into a nylon sack about the size of a Pop-Tart. He's wearing some kind of stretchy black shirt that conforms to his torso and highlights each individual muscle of his abs. Ellie scans him up and down, calls him Captain Hardwear, and asks if a cape comes with that outfit. Ceo explains that he didn't buy this stuff. He was in Montana on a catalog shoot for K2 Snowboards, and the booking agency gave Mountain Hardwear clothes to the models to keep them warm. Grahame and I know all about his trip to Montana last winter thanks to one especially long poker night when Ceo drank beers instead of Mountain Dews and won too much money. Usually he doesn't share intimate details, but on that particular night he went on and on. As soon as Ceo brought up Montana I knew Grahame would jump all over it—and he did.

"Tell her what else you did to stay warm," Grahame says with an edge to his voice. He's been trying to fasten the ax to the outside of his pack with bungee cords, and they keep coming unhooked whenever he stretches them.

"Yes," Ellie says. "I would very much like to hear what you poor models did to stay warm in Montana."

"Let's get to the top of this thing," Ceo says with a wink, "and maybe I'll show you."

"Shit!" Grahame says. One of the bungees popped loose and hit him in the face. There's an angry red welt on his cheek. An inch higher and we'd be looking at an empty socket.

Ceo says, "The bungees aren't happening, dude."

"They will."

"The ax is too heavy. Even if you get them to stay, it'll still flop around. Just leave it."

Grahame shakes his head. His face is tight, lips a thin hard line. I know this look. It's the same thing his opponents see across the net when he digs in and simply refuses to lose. And he never does. The only person that beats him at anything is Ceo, and when that happens, you'd think the world had stopped spinning and gravity was canceled. For whatever crazy reason, this ax is a line in the sand, and Ceo knows it.

Ceo says, "All right. If you won't leave it, then let's do this." He walks to the side of the parking lot, picks up a rock, tests the weight, drops it, picks up a bigger one. It takes two hands to lift it. He approaches Grahame, saying, "My pack has straps that will hold your ax. Since we're racing and I'll be hauling your extra weight, then you have to carry this to make it fair."

"*That* rock?"

Ceo nods.

"Why don't you give me some of your other weight? Like the tent and the stove?"

"Nah. It's this rock, or you carry that ax in your hand."

"You're serious?"

"Like zits on prom night."

"It's not a rock. It's a freaking boulder."

"When we get to the top, you can take it out. I'll still carry the ax."

"For the rest of the trip?"

"Right down to this spot."

I consider all the likely outcomes, and none of them are good for Grahame. Ceo set the hook at the visitor center. Now he's reeling him in. I say, "Leave it, Grahame. We'll be fine without it."

Grahame looks at Ellie. The welt below his eye is starting to leak red.

He says, "What about you, goalie girl?"

"I'm sorry. Were you talking to me?"

"Do you have an opinion to share?"

"I do. But you don't want to hear it."

Ceo holds out the rock. "Make the call, dude. My forearms are screaming."

Grahame slips on his sunglasses. Says, "Sure. Why not. I'll still beat your ass, and you know it." He takes the rock from Ceo, wedges it into the top of his pack. It bulges up and out like a big gray tumor. Ceo straps the ax to the side of his pack. We shoulder our loads; Grahame struggles a little putting his on. Then he locks up the Cherokee and we head for the Mirror Lake bus that is pulling up to the curb.

On the way Ellie asks me, "Are they always like this, or is it because I'm here?"

"Yes," I say. "And yes."

21
ELLIE

Grahame outmaneuvers Ceo and Colin to claim the seat next to Ellie. She wonders how this will play out as he struggles to wedge his pack between his huge legs, then gives a *snooze you lose* wave to his friends. They make their way to the remaining unoccupied seats, which are five rows back and across the aisle. As the bus pulls away and accelerates, Grahame says, "You think he played me."

"Like a drum."

"That's not the way I see it."

"What's your version?"

"I only carry that rock to the top. He'll be hauling the ax around for three days. Pound per mile, I have the better deal."

Until Ceo finds a way to get you to carry it. "But," she says, "what if this rock costs you your idiotic race and you have to be a DB or BB or whatever for two weeks."

"It's a BB, and I won't."

"Why not just leave the ax in the car?"

"It's . . ."—he glances back at Ceo and Colin—"personal."

"As in a comfort object? What's wrong with a stuffed bunny?"

He frowns. Takes a beat. "I'll tell you, but you can't laugh."

"I won't. Even if it's funny."

"First you have to put your hand on the sacred rock and make a solemn vow."

She puts her left hand on top of Grahame's pack.

Before she can react, his hand is on top of hers. It's big and rough, and it smothers hers like a hot blanket. Ellie's first instinct is to pull away. He presses down. Leans in very close and whispers warm in her ear, "Swear that you won't tell Ceo."

"I do so swear." *Now let me go.*

He regards her with those dark lenses. The cut from the bungee has stopped oozing. The drip of blood looks like a red tear. She tugs. He presses again.

"Uh, my hand . . ." she says. "It can't breathe."

He smiles and slides his off, like a sated thing. But not without a final reminder press. She tucks her hand under her right arm, resists the urge to wipe it off on her jeans.

What the hell was that about?

Grahame quietly says, "I'm afraid of bears."

"I don't believe you."

"No. I totally am. When I was a kid, I read a story in *Outside* magazine about a guy that was dragged out of his tent and mauled to death in front of his family. There was nothing they could do except listen to him scream. I had nightmares about it for months. Ever since then I've been afraid of bears. I won't see polar bears at the zoo. When my family took a road trip to Yellowstone and some bears were crossing the road, I hid on the floor behind the backseat and cried. Lions, snakes, great white sharks. None of them scare me. But bears . . ." He stares at his pack, fiddles with a strap. "I can't even look at their pictures in books."

"What about the Chicago Bears?"

"Not a fan."

"Koala bears?"

"Have you seen their claws?"

"Gummy bears?"

"Worst candy name ever."

"So you brought the ax for bear protection?"

"Correct."

"They have bear spray, you know. It comes in a can. Much lighter than an ax."

"I'm a tennis player. I need something to swing."

The bus pulls into a parking lot. A silence settles between them as passengers get off and on. She hopes that the seats across from her empty so Ceo and Colin can move up. They stay occupied. The bus starts moving and the driver announces the next stop is the Mirror Lake Trail. She glances back. Ceo is staring at them, his face a blank mask. Colin is looking up and out the window.

Grahame says, "You're not like his other girls."

"I'm not his girl. This is not an owner-slave relationship."

"See. That's one of my favorite things about you. You have actual thoughts."

"I'll take that as a compliment, and not a slam against my gender." Thinking *one* of his favorite things? Does that mean there are more? And that story about the bears. He said the words, acted the part. But he's too big and too strong. In a fight between Grahame and a bear, she's not so sure the bear would win.

The bus turns into another parking lot. It looks like the end of the line. The remaining passengers gather their stuff. She wants off this bus like it's on fire. Grahame sits there like he has all day.

He says, "I've been watching, you know."

"Watching what?"

"The way he looks at you."

"Is it good?"

"Yeah." A beat. "If you like train wrecks."

"Ceo's a big boy. He can handle himself."

Grahame lets out a laugh. It's deep and full and echoes through the emptying bus. "What's so funny?" she asks, forcing a smile as Ceo and Colin walk by.

He stands at last, unwedges his pack.

"Oooh, da goalie girl tinks I be talkin' about da Ceo."

22

COLIN

Ceo rips two pages containing a small map and trail description from the guidebook, tosses what's left of a twenty-five-dollar investment in the trash. He gives the pages to me with instructions to follow that trail past the lake, then a little ways after that cross a footbridge, then watch for a sign on the left pointing to the trail that goes up to Snow Creek Falls.

I ask, "Is this the only map you have?"

"I have a topo, but it's of Lower Merced Pass Lake. That's worthless now. Not to worry, though. The GPS is right here." He taps the front Velcro pocket on his pants. "We won't do anything tricky."

I think the tricky part has already started. Ellie is about twenty yards down the trail. She's snapping pictures of us, the trees in their autumn suits, and Half Dome, which is pretty much in our face.

Grahame says, "You ready to run, chief?"

"You know it."

"Have any final words for goalie girl?"

Ceo calls out, "Hey, Els! You want to count us down?"

She lowers her camera. "That would make me an accessory to murder."

"Then I'll see you in a couple hours."

"Good luck, Captain Hardwear."

Ceo and Grahame line up side by side with me between them facing down the trail, which at this point is paved and looks more like a road than a wilderness path leading to paradise. There are people ahead, taking their time, walking dogs, enjoying the scenery. They have no clue of the storm that's about to be unleashed behind them.

Grahame checks his watch. "One forty-eight. I'll be at the top by three fifteen."

Ceo says, "I'll have dinner ready when you get there."

They both give me a nod: Grahame with his knees flexed, torso bent forward at the hip, all tense and twitching like a greyhound on a leash; Ceo standing straight, arms hanging loose at his sides. They look like this every time we run bleachers. The big difference here are the refrigerators strapped to their backs.

I say, "You sure about this, guys? I mean, all the smoke. It could damage your lungs."

Grim silence is their answer.

I say, "And the tribe has spoken. On your mark. One . . . two . . ."

Grahame takes off like a fireball from a catapult.

Ceo shakes his head, says, "Why did I know he'd do that?"

He waves to me and Ellie, then leaves at an easy jog.

23
ELLIE

S he watches Ceo disappear around the bend, then decides it's time to stop putting off the inevitable. Colin waits while Ellie reads her texts.

JANICE BOYER

Dr. H called. You father is
so disappointed.

The Pepperdine coach wants
your cell number. Is that ok? ☺

PJ HAZELTINE

I'd love to chat. Call me when u get a min. Or see me after practice at 5.

Then her heart skips three beats.

CARL K BOYER

Mark said there is no record of your visit to Pepperdine!!!!!

JANICE BOYER

Where are you? Call me.

She sees a voice mail but chooses not to play it. Colin is six feet away, his eyes steady and focused on her. She thinks about calling her mother, but what would she say? That I'm about to walk into the wilderness with three guys and not to worry because one of them brought an ax? She would probably know Ceo because everyone knows his father. That wouldn't help at this stage, not with all the objects she set in motion. And then there's Colin, who at the moment is balancing a stick in the palm of his hand. Ellie decides her momentum is greater than the outside forces acting on it. She sets her phone on vibrate, buries it under her jacket in the top of her pack, and swings up the load.

Colin asks while she adjusts her shoulder straps, "Is something wrong?"

"Why do you ask?"

"You look like Ceo at a John Cusack film festival."

Ellie laughs despite the knot in her stomach. "I got a text from my mother. She's worried that I didn't have lunch."

"Lunch is a very important meal. Without lunch there would be no need to make sandwiches."

"Peanut butter would never have met jelly."

"Deals would go undone."

"Who wants to live in that kind of world?" she asks.

"Exactly. It's our duty to save the world. I hear there's a lake up ahead that looks like a mirror. We can mock our companions who are probably dead by now, while consuming dried strips of teriyaki-flavored cow muscle."

"My mother would be pleased."

They start walking side by side into the shadows of trees.

24
COLIN

Ellie snaps a few pictures of Mirror Lake, although it looks more like a pond to me. The trail description says it's been gradually shrinking over the years and isn't what it was back in the pre-drought days of John Muir and Ansel Adams. It isn't much of a mirror, either, with a cool wind picking up, rippling the surface and blurring the surrounding trees into an orange-yellow ring around the shore and turning the gray face of Half Dome silver. It's still breathtaking in a primordial-swamp kind of way. I feel the patient hand of nature filling in this body of water one fallen leaf at a time.

We shrug off our packs, open the jerky bag, and start chewing between sips of water. Our conversation up to this point has been Ellie telling me about her previous trips to Yosemite, twice with her family but they didn't camp out, once with four female soccer players from Germany that were staying at her home. I wonder how I can work in a question about her and Ceo and how that all started, but she preempts me by asking, "Why do they call you Q?"

I was hoping that subject wouldn't come up, but it invariably does. I'm thankful that she didn't ask it in front of Grahame, who goes into every possible detail and gets most of them wrong.

She says, "I'm sorry. If this is some man thing—"

"No, it's all right. The more I tell the story, the easier it gets."

"Ooh. There's a story?"

"Oh yes. And it deals with matters of personal hygiene and a virus, so if it gets too intense or you are easily offended..."

"I'll let you know if you cross any boundaries."

I say, "The story begins with me in my dorm room. Grahame has already left for class. I'm showered, teeth brushed, almost ready for school. I have a bio test in ten minutes and it's a seven-minute dash across campus. The problem is ever since I was a little kid I've had issues with waxy buildup in my ears."

"Waxy buildup? That sounds like a boundary issue to me."

"I know. But it's critical to the plot, so hang in there. Since the inside of my ears are still wet from the shower, I take a precious minute to clean them. At that exact moment I get a call on my cell."

"Is this where it gets interesting? Because so far I'm unimpressed."

"Coming right up. Fast-forward to just before the exam. I'm sitting in class, sweating from my cross-campus sprint and about to take a test that will have a forty percent impact on my final grade for the semester and possibly kill my scholarship at CGA." I pause, waiting to see if she's into this or not.

She says, "I'm all ears. Go on."

"That's when I get the famous Ceo text."

"You're lucky you got a text from him at all. But that's a different story. Tell me about this text."

Her brown eyes flared a little when she made the Ceo comment. I take a beat before saying, "It read, and I quote: 'Dude, you have a Q-tip in your ear. You're freaking famous!'"

It takes a moment for the truth to sink in. But when it does it hits her like a hammer.

"Oh my God! You're *that* guy!"

"The video was posted on the school blog, which was then reposted on every social network site known to man. By the end of the day the YouTube video had over twenty-five thousand hits. Q-tip Guy was born."

"My friend Nadia sent me the link. You made the Jimmy Fallon show. I remember he called it the worst example of product placement ever."

"Make one tiny mistake in personal hygiene and the whole world knows about it."

"So that's why you're familiar," she says. "But your hair was longer. And you had a ring in your ear. Fallon zoomed in a couple times."

"I cut my hair and lost the ring, which made my mother happy. So, anyway. There you have it. The story of Q-tip Guy, who now is known merely as Q." I stand, throw a rock at the mirror, and hope that it doesn't bring me bad luck. We put on our packs in silence.

As we're walking away from the lake Ellie says, "That must have been an important phone call."

I say, "Waxy buildup really sucks."

Ceo picks Colin up in the Mercedes outside his dorm. Says he doesn't want him riding his bike on their big challenge match day and wasting energy. Colin says it's only a ten-minute walk to class. Ceo says, No excuses. When I beat you, I want it to be your A game.

Speaking of energy and excuses, Colin smells perfume on the seat and asks Ceo when he got to bed last night because isn't that the same shirt you wore yesterday?

Ceo says, I didn't go to bed last night.

Colin asks if he went to bed at all.

We were in a bed, Ceo says. So technically, yeah.

He drives top down because that's what you do in SoCal on a morning like this, and Colin thinks about his night compared to Ceo's. While Ceo was sneaking around off campus doing whatever, probably with that girl with a name that rhymes with caffeine, or maybe it was the girl he met yesterday at the taco truck on Wilshire, Colin was trying to study for a philosophy test while Grahame kept interrupting with practice questions from the ASVAB.

Then he got the Mom call.

She said she was going through Dad's things in the garage and found that picture of you and him ice fishing the day you caught that big walleye. Do you want me to send it, since I'm going uptown anyway? It's a Tuesday morning, so there won't be a line at the Walmart.

Since it was 10:39 p.m. SoCal time, that meant it was 1:39 a.m. in Vermont. He knew it was a red flag, that she wasn't sleeping—still, after all these months, but what could he do from here? He could tell her no, please don't send it because it would hurt too much to open the box, so he probably wouldn't, at least not until finals were over. He could tell her she needs to go to sleep, maybe ask if she's taking the pills, but that would open another can of worms, and there isn't time. Not if he wants to finish studying and go to sleep at a reasonable hour. But he heard it in her voice, the backed-up ache of thirty years' planning for a future that ended in an instant. How could he even think about not talking with her?

I remember the day, he told her, stretching out on his bed and allowing a smile. Dad said I was fishing too deep. I brought up my line six inches, and when that fish hit, it almost yanked me into the hole. How old was I then?

You were eleven, she said. It was the same year we had all that flooding in the spring after Hurricane Lloyd. The Renkeys' dock broke loose, remember? They found it on the north shore up on the Holloways' deck. Dad towed it back and only charged him forty dollars, which of course didn't even cover the gas, not to mention three hours of his time.

Colin knew she had more to talk about, more about this day and the day before that and all the fragments of Dad's life still stuck in hers that have been reduced to details like what to keep and what to sell and what to give away. Today it's the fish picture. Last week it was the binoculars he gave him for Father's Day the year that Trevor Brandise broke his arm spearing pickerel. But Colin had a challenge match with Ceo the next day, and since Mom lit the Dad fuse, he wouldn't be able to concentrate on philosophy, so screw that, and he closed the book.

Colin? Are you there? she asked.

Yeah, I'm here, he said. Just thinking about that day. Dad got so excited, he slipped on the ice and bruised his hip.

She asked him again if he wanted her to send the picture. It would be no problem—in fact I even have it in a box and bubble-wrapped all ready to go.

Sure, he said. That would be nice. I'll show my friend Ceo. He's never even been fishing. And then he told her he needed to study for a philosophy final.

She said she understood and told him she loved him, to make good choices, and hung up.

The silence at the other end of the line was like an anvil on his chest.

Colin tried not to think about her alone in that house with all those boxes of Dad and rolls and rolls of Bubble Wrap.

He'd rather not think about it now.

So he focuses on Ceo turning left into student parking, feeling stupid for accepting a three-minute ride. As they're getting out of the car Colin asks him if he's still on for poker this Saturday.

Ceo says, Hell yeah. I'm always in the mood to take Grahame's money. But I can't next Saturday. My agent called last night with a thing, and I couldn't say no.

What thing is it this time? Colin asks.

Some kind of catalog shoot. A guy pulled out, so I'm in.

Where's it at?

San Clemente. Hey, you should come! I'll introduce you to the girls....

He leaves that hanging. The girls...As if Colin has a clue what to do with that.

Thanks but no, he says. I need to hit.

Q, this dry spell has gone on too long. It's depressing the shit out of me.

Colin says, You need to be thinking about the match this afternoon. That's where your focus should be.

He turns to leave for his class and the philosophy test he didn't study for.

Ceo says to him as he leaves, Remember, bring your A game. Nothing less. No excuses.

Colin thinks about the box headed his way.

Thinks about all that Bubble Wrap.

The same goes for you, he says.

And thanks him for the ride.

25
COLIN

After the lake, the crowd thins considerably. Once we fork left on the Snow Creek Trail, the crowd thins to exactly two. I thought there would be more people, since this is a weekend in prime foliage season. Back in Vermont, the hills would be crawling with hikers. I'm sure the smoke and threat of fire plays a role. Or maybe we got such a late start that everyone is already at the top, claiming the best camping spots.

Another possibility is they know something we don't and that's why it is just the two of us on this trail, plus the occasional crow or indifferent mule deer. The important fact for me is we are alone. Alone in a beautiful forest under a mostly blue sky, and neither one of us seems to be in a hurry.

I ask Ellie to tell me about her family. She says her father is an oncologist, currently doing research on immunotherapy treatments using different viruses, like polio, to stimulate the immune system into attacking cancerous tumors. She says the results are pretty amazing, and he's doing a presentation this weekend in Seattle. Her mother is an airline pilot, but she stopped flying three years ago to focus on Ellie's soccer. She has a twelve-year-old sister that loves gymnastics and dance and basically anything pink. Ellie has no pets at home (her sister has allergies), but after watching *Must Love Dogs* for the tenth time, she will have at least one dog as soon as she has her own place.

Ellie's voice helps distract me from the other voice in my head. The one that keeps whispering about this thing I read in the pages Ceo tore from the guidebook. He didn't mention it when he read the description to us outside the visitor center. Either he didn't see it (which I doubt because it was in bold), or he didn't think it was important (which I doubt because it was in bold). Either way, I feel the need to ask him if he got a wilderness permit. I don't see how that could happen unless he bought one at the visitor center, which I doubt because he spent all his time finding the guidebook.

The trail is too narrow to walk side by side, increasingly steep and rocky with great views but often with stomach-churning drop-offs. Ellie is in front setting the pace, which is steady and maybe even a little fast. I can tell she's an athlete by the way she moves. Even with a pack on Ellie dances around and over rocks, never looks off-balance, and has bottomless lungs. My quads are burning, and she just isn't slowing down. By my unofficial count we have thirty-five switchbacks down, seventy whatever to go.

Whenever we pass through a clearing, we scan the switchbacks above us. Once, we caught a glimpse of what could be Ceo and Grahame, but they were way up there and not moving very fast. A few minutes ago we heard what sounded like a yell echoing across the valley, and seconds after it, something crashed down through the trees about fifty yards to our right. I add rockfall to my growing list of concerns.

Plus there's my decision to leave the hiking boots in Vermont. I was standing in the garage staring at them on the shelf next to the box labeled IRRIGATION SUPPLIES, and couldn't pull the trigger. Now my right tennis sneaker has a dime-size hole where I drag my toe when I serve. The duct tape I used to cover the hole fell off somewhere between here and the lake. When a pebble slips in, which it often does, I have to shake my leg till it pops out. Most of the time it works. Not this time.

I ask Ellie to stop.

She waits at the top of the next switchback, glazed with sweat and sipping from her blue water bottle. I slip twice on the smooth granite covered with gravel on my way up to where she's standing, then shake my leg one more time, trying in a vain attempt to dislodge the stone wedged under my big toe. She hands me her water bottle and asks, "Are you having a seizure?"

I take three grateful hits, give it back to her. She tops it, stows the bottle in her pack, and waits while I kick off my sneaker and dump out the pea-size stone. The trail has already worn an embarrassing hole in my recently new sock.

Lacing up my shoe, which isn't that easy with a pack on, I say, "These are my lucky Nikes. In case you're wondering."

"They look pretty lucky," she says.

"I would have worn my fancy boots like yours. But then I wouldn't have any luck."

"Why do you need luck?"

"That's the thing about luck. You never know when you'll need it. For example, it would be very lucky if you had duct tape in your pack."

"Sorry. I had to choose between tape and toilet paper. At least they're both on rolls."

I'm framing my response when voices from above cut me short. We look up and see three men wearing packs making their way down. It takes a couple minutes for them to reach us. All of them are older, easily in their forties, one with a green do-rag and impressive beard dripping sweat, another with trekking poles, which I openly eye with envy. The last one has gray hair spilling out from under a GO NAVY cap. He's the oldest by far, maybe even in his sixties, but tall, lean, and barely breaking a sweat. Navy Guy is the one who asks us where we're headed.

Ellie looks at me like *yeah, sport, where are we headed?*

"To the top of this. After that I think we're going to either Tenaya Lake, or maybe climb North Dome, or do the Yosemite Falls loop." I sound like I know what I'm talking about, but really I don't. It's straight from the pages in my pocket and the trail descriptions Ceo read aloud in the parking lot.

Navy Guy, after a lingering look at my shoes, says, "Those are all good options. I did North Dome in February last year. Great views once the storm cleared." He nods toward the ridge. "Where're y'all spending the night?"

"We'll probably hike in a ways, then look for a spot."

"How many nights?"

"Two."

Navy Guy's brows gather in concern. He looks past me, scans the sky toward the west. I can tell he's about to say something when his buddy with the poles says, "Do you folks have a bear canister?"

"No," I say, not even knowing what that is and not liking the sound of it. "Is there a problem?"

He grunts. "Yeah. A three-hundred-pound problem."

Navy Guy says, "I was taking these guys on the Clouds Rest loop, but a bear got most of our food last night. Turned a three-day trip into an overnighter."

Do-rag adds, "I guess he's a pretty nasty one. We ran into a couple like you on their way down yesterday. They tried to scare him off with whistles and spray, but that didn't go so well. He wiped them out, too."

Navy Guy says, "Y'all better do a good job hanging your food. Better than us, anyway. An' I thought we did a damn good job." Unsmiling nods from his friends. "But you know how it goes. If a bear wants your food, he's gonna get it."

No. I actually *don't* know how *it* goes. My experience camping in the Green Mountains of Vermont never included a wild animal encounter other than a moose, and it was on the other side of a lake. I look at Ellie, wondering how this development works for her. She smiles at my *oh shit* expression and says to me, "Don't worry. Ceo will probably talk it into bringing us a trout." Then to the three men, "Speaking of determined animals, our friends are ahead of us. Maybe you saw them? They'd be the crazy ones running up the trail."

Navy Guy frowns. "Those two yay-hoos are with y'all?"

"They're racing."

"Well, that figures. I've seen some crazy shit in my navy days, but running up this trail wearing full packs? I'm gonna say that bypasses crazy and goes straight to dumb as a stump."

Sweaty Beard says, "We heard them before we saw them. I thought, Shit, it's *another bear*. Then we saw them two switchbacks below us—*running*! The guy in back was trying to pass the guy in front. The guy in front moved like he was trying to knock the other guy off the trail."

"He did not do that," the other friend protests. "It was incidental contact."

"Of course you say that, Darryl. That's how you play hoops. Everything is incidental. Even if you hacked off a limb, you'd still call it *incidental*." Darryl smiles and shrugs. "So anyway, back to what really happened. We lose track of your pals in the trees. Hear a kind of yell-scream . . ." He pauses while I trade troubled glances with Ellie. "Then it's just one of them on the next switchback. No sign of the other guy. We're thinking, Oh shit, what happened to him? Did he get knocked off the trail or what?"

Ellie drinks from her bottle. "I'm confused. Which one are you talking about now?"

"The blond guy carrying the ax. He was the one that was trying to pass. Except now he's all alone. He jogs up to us, stops for a second, barely breathing hard, and asks if we could please check on his friend. Said he wasn't looking too good. Then he jogs on up the trail. We're thinking this is a little unusual but okay, whatever—"

"Maybe you've figured it out by now," Darryl says, leaning against his poles. "Charlie's the talker in our family."

Ellie says, "Keep talking, Charlie."

"So we walk down to check on his friend. He's sitting on a boulder, face as red as your shirt." He points to Ellie. "Boy, does he look *pissed*! I'm talking the red-faced and frothing kind of pissed. Then *get this*. He rips off his pack. Opens the top. Hauls out what had to be a goddamn *twenty-pound rock*! You know, like, isn't his pack *heavy enough already*? Then he yells, excuse my French: *FUCK THIS FUCKING ROCK!* and hurls it over the side." Charlie shakes his head, freeing a couple more drips of sweat. "Un-freaking-*believable*."

I say, "You'd be surprised how freaking believable that is." I'm pretty certain based on Ellie's nervous glance up at the rim that she's thinking what I'm thinking. Grahame and Ceo alone together is not a good thing right now. "Thanks for the update," I say. "We'd better go."

Ellie puts her water bottle away.

Charlie says, "Hang on a sec, I haven't gotten to the good part yet."

"There's a good part?" I ask.

"Hell yeah. So we give him some Gatorade and a granola bar, stay with him a couple minutes until his breathing settles down and his color comes back. He thanks us for the help, says he's good to go, mon, in some kind of accent. Then my dad," he says, looking at Navy Guy, "opens his mouth like usual and says this stupid thing."

"What did you say?" Ellie asks Navy Guy.

"I warned him about the bear."

"How did that go?"

"Not so good," Navy Guy says, his gray eyes smiling. "Y'all's friend threw up that Gatorade and peanut butter granola bar all over Charlie's boots."

*   *   *

They're driving back from a tournament in Burlington where Colin lost in the semis to a kid from Stowe he beat last summer. Either the kid improved or Colin got worse, because it was basically a 6-1, 6-2 blowout. Colin nervous behind the wheel, ready to talk about anything other than the match, or nothing at all, which would work, too. But his father likes to fill empty silences with buckets of words.

He starts by asking Colin for an update on his boss at the hatchery, does he still think that Champ, Lake Champlain's version of the Loch Ness Monster, is real and eating all the perch? Which somehow morphs, as all conversations eventually do these days, into whether or not Colin should bail on that Chandler Gates school in California because that doesn't seem to be shaping up like we all hoped. Colin knows he's right. That decision has to be made, but letting go of this particular dream is a reality he's not ready to face. Consequently the conversation doesn't go so well for either of them, leading to a silence that even his father can't fill. They stare out at all the green under gathering clouds with low black bellies promising a dump that Colin wishes had come two hours earlier. Lightning flashes down to treetops in the distance.

His father says, Take this exit.

Colin asks why.

He says it's time to address the endless residues of life.

I don't know what that means, Colin says.

His father says, You've been wanting to do this one thing for a long time. And I've been letting all those residues pile up and get in the way.

Stop talking dad code, Colin says, taking the exit and pulling up to a stop sign. Cows huddle in a pasture across the road, tails twitching at flies in the humid calm. Colin waits because he doesn't know which way to turn.

Go right, his dad says.

Colin asks, So what's this about?

He says, It's about time we do that thing you always wanted to do.

Colin makes the turn, asking, Which thing is that?

His dad says, Let's ski Tuckerman Ravine.

And then the sky opens like it was slashed with a claw, dropping a warm torrent while the car rocks in the sudden wind, and Colin hits the wipers but they can't keep up. As the sky flashes silver and thunder rolls, he makes that turn, thinking that one dream dies so another can live, and how the timing of this storm couldn't be more perfect.

They walk out of Leatherman's Gear and Tackle with two new pairs of one-hundred-dollar hiking boots, the kind his father says they need to do Tuckerman right. During the drive home they make plans to leave for New Hampshire in two weeks because any later and the snow might be gone. Colin will have to skip the tournament in Plattsburgh and maybe the one in Killington, too. That's okay, they agree, because since California isn't working out, this is the bigger deal.

When they drive into the garage, Mom meets them at the door, waving an actual envelope, which she hands to Colin. He sits on the riding lawn mower and tears into the envelope while his father fiddles with a fishing pole, his mother knocks down a spiderweb, and the car drips. The letter is from Coach Carson at Chandler Gates Academy in Los Angeles, saying the Lyle Gates Scholar Athlete Award is currently available and it's his if he makes the top two and maintains a 3.7 or better GPA.

The one-hundred-dollar hiking boots go onto the shelf next to a crate marked IRRIGATION SUPPLIES.

That's where they stay untouched until Colin flies home for the funeral ten months later, when he pulls them down, thinks about taking them back to LA, but decides no.

Too much weight.

26

COLIN

Fifteen minutes and eight switchbacks after saying happy trails to the three men, we pass a pool of drying vomit. It attracted a cloud of flies we heard buzzing twenty feet away. The trail is too narrow to get by without coming uncomfortably close to the edge of a serious drop-off. Our only choice is to step over the brown-and-white-flecked stain and through the flies, holding our breath against the sour air as we go. Once we're on the other side and safely beyond the smell, Ellie stops and asks the question I've been expecting ever since Ceo and Grahame made their bet in the parking lot this morning.

"What's a Double-B?"

"It's not pretty."

"That's a given. Tell me the gory details."

I explain how Grahame and Ceo wanted an alternative currency for bets that didn't involve real money, since Ceo had too much, Grahame had some, and I didn't have any. They created the Double-B, aka Bag Boy, in which the loser of the bet has to carry the winner's racquet bag for the entire day and fill his water bottle when needed.

"Seriously?" she says. "Isn't tennis competitive enough already? Do you have to demean the people that actually provide this service for a living?"

"We never bet on tennis," I say, aware that I only answered the first half of her question and avoided the second half entirely because it is demeaning and stupid and there really is no excuse. On the other hand, looking at her leaning a little forward on her walking stick, I'm also keenly aware of how some people work the sweaty T-shirt look better than others.

Ceo is good. Ellie is better.

She turns and resumes walking. I expect her to ask the obvious question, *Has Ceo or Grahame ever been a bag boy?* To which I would answer no and yes respectively, and that's a major bone of contention. Instead she asks me if I've been a victim of that ridiculous bet.

I say, "Almost."

"Why almost?"

"I lost a bet to Ceo."

"What was the bet?"

"A regrettable decision involving a seagull and a homeless man. In the end it doesn't matter because Ceo offered me clemency if I did this one thing."

"Did you accept?"

"I did."

"What was the one thing?"

"I had to go on a catalog shoot with him."

"Sounds humbling. Where was it?"

"San Clemente."

After a beat. "When was that?"

"Two weeks ago."

She takes another beat. And another. Says, "I had a soccer tournament in San Clemente."

"When?"

"Two weeks ago."

I say nothing, wondering about this new puzzle piece and how it fits.

She asks, "Did you go?"

"No."

"Why not?"

"There was an unfortunate event at school. It caused me to reject my clemency."

"Well. That's . . . unfortunate."

We walk in silence for a bit. Then I can't help but ask, "While you were playing soccer in San Clemente . . ."

"Yes?"

"Did you happen to spy any blond tennis players with bad acting skills wearing a John Cusack Sucks T-shirt?"

27

ELLIE

"No," she says, her mind wheeling. "But an old man on Rollerblades asked me to autograph his Speedo."

"Cool. Front or back?"

"Always go with the back. Less bumpy."

"I'll file that under information I wish I didn't know."

Their conversation stalls after that, which is okay with her. She needs the time to sort through this San Clemente revelation and what it means, if anything at all. It could be the universe flexing its random muscle, but she doubts it. The odds are much higher that Ceo is up to something. After a couple more switchbacks, Colin says he needs another pebble stop. She finds a place with a decent sitting rock and unwraps a chocolate bar while he takes off and dumps his shoe. During this process he says, "So you play on the U-18 national team?"

"Played. How did you know that?"

"Ceo told us. He said you had a shutout against Brazil in Barcelona."

Ellie considers the source of this information. She knows she didn't tell Ceo about the national team while they were at the workshop because she didn't tell anyone. He must have googled her, which would result in links to USsoccer.com and her high school website, both of which feature articles about her and her tournament schedule. This means he's been paying attention to her when she thought he wasn't. The randomness of San Clemente is feeling incrementally less random.

She says, "Actually, I had two shutouts if you don't count the own goal in the semifinals."

Finished with his shoe, he sits on the rock next to her. She hands him the chocolate bar. He breaks off a piece and offers her some of his water. "The national team. That's crazy."

"*Crazy* is a good word."

"Are you the next Hope Solo?"

She smiles. There aren't many guys her age that know that name. "Not if I can help it."

"Why? Are you a Hope hater?"

"No. I'm a soccer hater."

"There's a twist I didn't see coming."

"It's a twisty kind of day."

"Is there a reason for this soccer rage?"

"There is. But I'd rather not talk about it now."

They eat and drink in silence while watching a hawk do slow, lazy turns on a late-afternoon thermal. Colin asks, "Before we move on to something else, just to be safe . . . what other topics are on Ellie's love-to-hate list that I should avoid?"

"Cigarette butts. They take ten months to ten years to biodegrade and are a fire hazard. Why isn't that considered littering? Sequels to movies that shouldn't have been a movie in the first place. Why is there a market for *Piranha Six*? And number one on my all-time love-to-hate list: elephant poachers. Don't get me started on them."

"I won't. But now you have me worried."

"About what?"

"What is your position on egg poachers?"

"Please do not tell me you are an egg poacher."

He nods sadly.

She snatches the chocolate bar from him in feigned anger. "I knew there was something sinister about you. Why do all the good guys I meet turn out to be poachers?"

"It's not my fault. I was forced into the life."

"That's what they all say."

"But it's true. My mother's favorite food is eggs Benedict. That's what my father and I used to cook for her every Mother's Day. And my father...he...he liked poached perch eggs in cream on toast. By the time I was old enough to see the horror, I was in too deep."

"Well," she says, noting the different tenses of his parents, "who doesn't like a creamy platter of poached perch eggs now and then?"

The hawk banks right and heads west. They watch it fade into the horizon, which has become increasingly gray. It triggers a thought that feels like it should be important, but it isn't quite there, so she leaves it for later, bumps Colin with her shoulder, and says, "It's your turn now. Tell me what's on your love-to-hate list."

"War and starvation?"

"Nope. I gave you something original. Something about me. You have to do the same. Give me something that is distinctly Colin-esque."

He turns from the void, his eyes seeking and finding hers. She hasn't seen him quite like this, feels a subtle change in the wind of him. He returns to the void.

"Bubble Wrap," he says. "Definitely not a fan."

They go off campus to buy pulled-pork burritos for lunch, two bottled waters plus a deluxe side of jalapeño fries with extra chipotle sauce to share, then cross the street to a small shady park overlooking the beach. Ceo brings the Frisbee in case there's time for a toss, but the burrito line was longer than usual, so that's not in the cards. Unless Colin decides to bail on his one thirty class. Ceo says that's the obvious play, given the babe-to-wave ratio is plus two point five, and we're playing a challenge match at three, and, Q, you're gonna need all your brainpower for that.

As they walk to an open table Ceo stops to regard a homeless man they observed while standing in line. He was working the garbage cans, reaching all the way down to his shoulder. Now he's horizontal on a bench, knit cap folded over his eyes, and one dark arm hanging down to the grass. The scent of garbage around him competes with car exhaust and fry grease and salt from the ocean breeze. A seagull is perched on the bench at the man's feet, which are sockless in unmatched shoes without laces. The bird is eyeing the remains of a sandwich still in the man's curled fingers with one thumbnail as black as oil. Colin moves to scare the bird away, but Ceo says, Wait, it's man vs. nature. He bets Colin a Double-B that the bird scores the sandwich before the homeless dude wakes up. Colin agrees to the wager against his better judgment because that's how it goes when your friend is a force of that very same nature.

Plus that friend paid for the fries.

After talking about Coach's latest agility drills that suck almost as much as running bleachers, and whether or not Rhody has a serious online poker habit warranting intervention, Ceo takes a long pull on his water and nods to the bird that hasn't moved a feather. He snaps a picture with his Samsung and says, Q, looks like you're finally gonna win one.

Colin says, You think I should call 911?

Ceo says, Nah, he's just taking a bench nap. And it wouldn't be fair to the bird that has invested all this time. Before Colin can calculate how sick that statement is on how many levels, Ceo asks him why he was so quiet on the drive this morning. You had something on your mind and I know it wasn't Meno's Paradox.

Colin stirs the chipotle sauce with a fry.

Ceo says, You got the Mom call, right?

Colin nods, eats the coated fry. Knows it's too late to steer the conversation back to safer ground.

Ceo asks if she's sending another package.

Yes, Colin says. A picture of me with a big fish.

Is your dad in this picture?

No. He took the photo. We were in an ice-fishing tournament for walleyes.

Ceo laughs. Asks, What the hell's a walleye?

It's a cross between a perch and a pike.

There's actually tournaments to catch walleyed fish through the ice?

Winters in Vermont are too long, Colin tells him. We have to do something.

Ceo asks, Will you even open this package? Grahame says you haven't opened the last three.

Colin says, They'll get opened. Not before midterms, though.

Ceo consumes the last fry, glances at man vs. nature. The standoff rages on.

He says to Colin, Why don't you just ask her to stop sending those packages until you're ready?

Because she needs to send them more than I need her to stop.

Because the residues of life would pile up and bury her.

Because she has miles and miles of Bubble Wrap.

But Colin doesn't say any of that.

Because Ceo's eyes go wide, and he whispers, Dude, it's game on!

The seagull is perched on a kneecap. The man's hanging arm twitches. The bird flaps its wings and rises up with a shriek, Colin thinking, Yes, I won. Then thinking, No I didn't, as the seagull wheels around, swoops down, snatches that sandwich from the man's fingers, and heads toward the beach with its crusty prize.

The man goes fetal but does not wake up.

Ceo grins at Colin, says, Lesson one, never bet against nature, so it looks like I have a bag boy for our match.

Colin says, Looks like you do, and wonders if this is all some elaborate ploy to mess with his mind before they face off across the net in less than two hours.

They toss their garbage and turn to leave.

Colin holds his breath and puts the uneaten half of his burrito on the man's backpack. Ceo slips a twenty under the flap. As they walk to the car Ceo says with the Frisbee spinning on his finger like a top, You know, Q, I'll grant you clemency on the bet if you go on the gig with me.

What gig?

I told you this morning. The catalog shoot in San Clemente.

Ah, that one. Will I get to see your muscles oiled up and glistening in the sun? I just can't get enough of that.

Yeah, well, it's the price of admission, Ceo says. On the bright side, chances are all the bikini-clad models will block your view.

Colin gets into the Mercedes, still smells perfume on the leather from last night.

He thinks about the role the seagull played in this decision he's about to make.

Ceo says, Well, what's the verdict?

Colin says, All right, as long as I don't have to see your greasy six-pack for hours on end.

Ceo pulls away from the curb into traffic, shouting over "Wu-Tang Clan Ain't Nuthing Ta F' Wit." You, my blue-balled amigo, are gonna break out of your love slump. You're gonna meet the girl of your sweet dreams in San Clemente, California!

Oh man, he can fuckin' feel it.

28

COLIN

We find Grahame sitting on a rock in the late-afternoon sun. The top can't be more than a few switchbacks away, yet here he is. He smiles as we approach, like it's all good. Like nothing happened and it's just him resting his legs while enjoying this fine view. But I know Grahame. He can be the picture of serenity on the outside and tossing hand grenades at seal pups on the inside. Something happened between him and Ceo on this trail, and how he feels about that something is a mystery. But it won't be one of those reveal-on-your-deathbed kinds of mysteries. In fact, I bet this mystery won't last five minutes because I saw the private look he shot me when Ellie was snapping a picture. We wait while he shoulders his pack, then nods to Ellie and says, "Your lead, goalie girl." We start up the remaining switchbacks single file with Grahame taking my place behind her.

At the first turn he says, "Q, no wonder it took you so long to get up here. I'd be taking my sweet time if I had this to look at all day."

"Keep your eyes on the trail, mister," Ellie says, "or you may find yourself at the bottom of it."

Grahame laughs.

At the second turn he says, "Ellie, did Q tell you how he got his name?"

"Yes."

"Almost one point five million viewers last time I checked. Dude's more famous than the penguin that plays blackjack. Pretty amazing, huh?"

"Not really, considering the depravity of YouTube."

"Did he tell you what Ceo stands for?"

"No."

"Good. Then I can tell you. His dad named him Ceo because he wants him to take over the family business and build megamalls just like him. It stands for chief executive officer."

"Colin, add another hate to my list. Parents that name their kids after acronyms."

"It's on my list, too," I say.

"Do you know what CEO *really* stands for?" Grahame asks.

"No," Ellie says. "And I'm pretty sure I don't want to."

At the last turn, with Ceo beaming down at us from the top, Grahame says, "I came up with it all by myself while I was waiting for you guys. It stands for *Cheats. Everyone. Often.*"

And there you have it.

With thirty-five seconds to spare.

We know why Ceo won.

Cheats. Everyone. Often.

I like it.

29

COLIN

C eo says you have to see this, you just *have* to see it.

We follow him on mercifully level ground through pine trees to a spot off the main trail looking out over the valley. He walks to a place that looks like the edge of the world, then six feet from that edge pretends to trip on a root and skid to a stop inches from falling into the abyss—which gets a laugh from exactly no one. But we're all too tired and in actual awe of the view to be pissed.

Half Dome has been our constant companion during the climb, but at this moment, with the sun hanging low like it is and the shadows angling the way they are, I can't imagine Mother Nature putting on a better display than she is right now. Ceo reminds us that we're looking at the largest mound of exposed granite in the world, then says, at this this very moment, in the presence of these witnesses, he vows to put climbing the face of her on his bucket list. Personally I just wish he'd stop hanging out so close to the edge. There's loose gravel on the smooth rock where he stands, and a gusting wind is making the pine trees restless. The end result is my stomach getting a bad case of the creeping willies. And then there's Grahame. He hasn't spoken since we reached the top except what he just whispered to me after Ceo made his vow:

Bucket list, hell. All he's got is a fuck-it list.

We spend a few minutes snapping pictures, the men with their phones and Ellie with her camera trying different lenses. I only take one pic because my phone officially died on the second. Ceo hands me his phone, which I notice has three solid bars and a battery at 75 percent. He asks me to take a picture of him and Ellie with Half Dome behind them. Then Grahame says he wants a picture of the three of us. He tells us to squeeze closer so he can fit that mountain into the shot. Then with the wind pushing us backward, the ground starting to slope gently down, and that two-thousand-foot drop somewhere behind us, he says to back up a little, a little more, a little more. We hit the gravel close to the edge. Ellie tenses beside me. I'm one heartbeat from telling Grahame this isn't funny when Ceo says, "This is far enough, take the damn picture already."

We gather a little ways off the trail to discuss our plans for the next two days. We're ten yards from a clear stream, which I remember from the map is Snow Creek. It's hard to believe this gentle water is the source of the thundering waterfall we heard earlier today. I know that if Dad were here, he'd be drifting a fly through that pool in the shade next to the big flat rock. We'd be eating trout for dinner tonight, not the mac 'n' cheese Ceo bought at Ralphs, four boxes for $2.99.

Ceo has the map out and talks while he shows us how we can go straight, then hook around and climb North Dome tomorrow, then loop back to the valley by hooking up with the Yosemite Falls Trail.

We'd camp somewhere around Yosemite Creek tomorrow night. The other option is to fork right, climb Mount Watkins tomorrow, and camp on the summit at 8,500 feet, which he says would be all kinds of awesome, or just have a snack on top, then head for either Tenaya Lake or Hidden Lake and camp there. We'd get up bright and early the next morning and head home via the same killer trail we did today. Ellie asks him what he thinks we should do.

Ceo folds and pockets the map. "I talked to a couple of trail-maintenance guys that were just leaving when I got here. They said there is no trail up Watkins, but the north side is a relatively easy scramble through bushes, then up granite slabs, but you don't want to be doing it in the dark. So I vote we tank up on water, then fork right and camp on top of Watkins tomorrow."

Grahame says, "Sounds cool. I've never slept on top of a mountain."

"What about the weather?" Ellie asks. "I heard there may be a storm heading this way."

"Where'd you hear that?" Ceo asks.

"I called someone while I was in the visitor center. He said San Francisco was going to get slammed this weekend."

"Well, I checked the weather just before you guys got up here, and Yosemite looks good till Saturday night or Sunday morning. From what I saw, the storm was moving more north than east. We'll know by tomorrow afternoon. If it looks bad, we turn around. I hope everyone brought gloves because it's going to get cold."

Grahame and Ellie nod. I brought gloves, but they're my work gloves from cleaning tennis courts. Old, leather, and not very warm.

"How good is your signal?" Ellie asks.

"Three bars, solid."

"What about the GPS?" Grahame asks.

"Working fine."

Ellie asks me about my phone.

I say, "Officially dead."

We all turn to Grahame. He shakes his head, says, "Unless I'm standing under a tower, I'd be better off with pigeons."

This leads to a moment of collective silence. When we hatched this crazy plan at the poker game, Ceo suggested we go old-school and do it off the grid. No phones, no GPS. That was voted down three to one. Looks like we're mostly there anyway.

I ask Ceo, "Where are we camping tonight?"

"I think there's about an hour of decent light left. We still need to set up camp and make dinner, so I suggest we find a spot around here. I thought it would be crowded, but we've got the place pretty much to ourselves. Plus I don't know about you guys, but I don't feel like putting on that pack."

"No way we're camping here," Grahame says.

"Why not?"

"If you stopped and talked to those people coming down the trail, instead of using them to *cheat*, then you'd know about the bear."

Ceo's eyes hardened when Grahame used the *C* word. I braced for a possible eruption because Ceo doesn't take to being called a cheater (although he doesn't mind calling other people cheaters). After a moment he says, "What bear?"

"The one chasing all the campers away."

"Seriously? Big bad Grahame is worried about a bear? Yosemite bears are like overgrown chipmunks."

"Chipmunks don't eat *flesh*, dude. Bears are like sharks with legs. They smell blood from miles away. It's like a freaking dinner bell to them." And he shoots Ellie a quick look. His intensity is surprising. This isn't a joke to him. He's vibrating, and Ceo knows it.

Ceo says, "Are you planning on skinning a deer?"

"No."

"Do you have a rib eye in your pack?"

"No, but—"

"So I don't see a problem camping here."

"Maybe you don't see a problem, but I do. And you should, too, because depending on what time of the month"—he gives Ellie another look—"you may want to think about sleeping in a tree."

Ceo says to Grahame, "*Time of the month?* Did you really say that?"

"She's been using the bathroom a lot."

"Meaning what?"

"I've said enough. Ask her."

"I'm not asking her because *A*, that period thing with bears is bullshit and *B*, it's none of my business, and it certainly isn't any of yours."

"Then I'll ask her."

"Go ahead. I hope she clubs you with her stick."

Grahame says to Ellie, "Is it, you know, that time of month?"

She looks him straight in the eyes and flexes her fingers around the stick.

Then with just the hint of a smile she says, *"Barely, mon."*

We spend ten minutes topping off our water bottles with filtered water from Snow Creek, then we're packs on again, walking single file in and out of the trees with gray-topped mountains all around. Ceo is up front talking cameras with Ellie. He's still carrying the ax and hasn't said a word about it or the fact that Grahame is his bag boy for two weeks. He also hasn't reacted to Grahame saying that he cheated on the climb, but I know Ceo heard it, and I know it stuck in a bad way. And I know Grahame won't stop picking at that scab.

Grahame is hanging back just a little behind Ellie. She switched to sweatpants over her shorts, which I'm sure disappointed him but not enough to give up his spot. That's okay because the closer we get to setting up camp, the more distance I want to put between her and me. My mind keeps conjuring up images of Ceo crawling into his tent and zipping up the door with Ellie's backlit silhouette showing through the nylon. I'll have Grahame snoring beside me, so I expect it will be a very long night.

Shortly after forking right we come to a small footbridge that crosses Snow Creek. They keep walking. I stop in the middle to remember this spot, knowing that if I listen, I'll hear one of my father's favorite sounds, clear water moving over and around rock. I have to listen pretty hard because the wind is picking up, even here with the trees to slow it down.

A finger of cold blows through my shirt, reminding me that what

I'm wearing now is wet and that I left a perfectly dry and warm hoodie in the Cherokee. I shiver, wishing I could have that decision over again, then look up at the treeless dome of Mount Watkins and wonder what a night will be like up there.

Ceo yells, "Q! It's time to say good-bye to Bear-topia."

Under a sky the color of orange flames, I cross the bridge.

30

COLIN

Ceo stops to check his GPS.

"We've gone far enough in this direction," he says. "Let's look for a spot to set up the tents."

"Which way now, chief?" Grahame asks.

Ceo steps off the trail on the Watkins side. "We may as well get a start on tomorrow," and leads us into the woods.

After twenty minutes of meandering up a gradual slope, we come to a spot where the ground has been worn away, exposing a slab of relatively flat rock. It's big enough to accommodate our tents plus have room for a fire. The wind isn't too bad here, which is a huge plus, but this rock won't offer much comfort to someone without a sleeping pad. A little farther up the slope there's a fallen tree leaning against a big boulder. It could come in handy for firewood, seeing as we just happen to have an ax.

We drop our packs with appreciative groans, then it's a frenzied search for our headlamps and something warm to wear because darkness is falling like a brick and brings with it a cold so sharp that it feels like teeth. I slip into the warmest thing I have, a nylon jacket with a thin flannel lining, and zip the collar all the way up to my chin. It hardly makes a dent in the cold, but that could be because I'm still wearing my sweaty T-shirt. I look at Ellie. She's dressed in a fleece jacket, gloves, and a knit ski hat with earflaps. She's staring at her phone while her breath clouds and swirls in the beam of her headlamp. She slips her phone into her pack and closes the top. I shift my gaze upward, see early stars shining in a purple-black sky with the promise of more stars to come. Good, I think. No clouds. Hopefully, Ceo is right and the storm is moving north.

Ellie says, "I need to use the restroom," and aims her headlamp at that boulder about sixty yards up the hill.

"Don't forget to flush," Ceo says. He pulls a small folding shovel from his pack. She takes the shovel and starts walking, scanning the ground with her light as she goes.

Grahame calls after her, "Need someone to stand guard?"

"What I really need is someone to build a fire."

Grahame grabs the ax, which is leaning against Ceo's pack. He starts following Ellie.

"Where are you going?" Ceo says.

"Woman want fire. Me chop wood."

31

ELLIE

Ellie starts walking up the hill with a shovel in hand, thinking about her phone and the news it shared and didn't share. There were three voice mails, none of them picked up. No service. And one text that must have arrived while she was at the lake with Colin.

NADIA

> Your mom is calling everyone asking where you are. I told her I don't know. You owe me huge. BTW where are u?

She hears footsteps behind her moving up the easy slope, figures it might be him, hopes it's anyone but. She looks back and says, "I told you I don't need a guard."

Grahame says, "I want to tell you I'm sorry."

"And I'm supposed to believe you?"

"It's the truth."

"Is that why you have the ax? To convince the nonbelievers?"

Walking beside her now, he says, "You said you want a fire." He aims his beam at the tree. "There's the wood."

"Apologies and axes don't mix."

"Why are you making this so hard for me?"

"Because you make it so hard not to."

They reach the tree. The dead branches, in the shadows from their lights, look like a tangle of broken ribs around a mossy spine. She realizes the boulder isn't as big as it looked from camp, and doesn't like the prospect of Grahame doing his thing while she's ten feet away, pants down, squatting over a hole in the dark. If Nadia were here, she'd give Ellie a told-you-so frown then ask, *How's Newton's law working for you now?* Ellie glances back at the camp. One headlamp is busy setting up a tent. The other is standing still, facing them.

Grahame says, "So, anyway. About that apology. I'm sorry about asking you if it's that time of month. It really isn't my business."

"Your comment about dinnertime for sharks was especially charming."

"Yeah. My bad there, and I'm sorry."

His tone is right. He sounds like he means it, but she can't see his eyes through the glare of his headlamp. She softens her voice a little and says, "How about if we make a deal? I'll accept your apology if you give me some privacy?"

Grahame nods. "Okay. But I have something else to say."

"Make it quick." And shows him the shovel. "I have a hole to dig."

"I want to thank you for not telling Ceo about my problem with bears. You could have said something, but you didn't."

"I was tempted. But you asked me not to on the bus, so I bit my tongue instead."

"I was thinking maybe there was a different reason."

"No. That's pretty much it," she says.

"You know what I was thinking about when I was sitting alone on that rock in the sun?"

How Ceo left you in the dust on the trail.

"I do not," she says. "And I really need to—"

"I was thinking about you and Ceo. How he doesn't seem to be spending a lot of quality time with you. The more I thought about it, the more it just doesn't make sense."

"What doesn't make sense?"

"You and him. I've seen the girls he dates. They're basically three types. Models, former models, and future models. You're not any of those."

"What does that mean?" She tightens her grip on the shovel. Her thoughts equally divided between hitting him over the head with it, and wanting to hear his twisted version of an answer to a question that's been nagging her ever since the second day at the workshop. When Ceo asked her to be his project partner over all the other future starlets that worked so hard to corner his affection.

Grahame says, "I think one of you has a bad case of dater's remorse. It could be because you're smart enough to see through his endless bullshit. But my money is on Ceo, who is basically a dick with legs." Then he moves in another step. The ax handle bumps against her thigh. "He doesn't see how . . . how *amazing* you really

are. But I can, Ellie. From the minute I saw you at the airport."
He smiles. "I thought, there's someone that finally sees him for
who he really is. So here's my theory. I think he's date-dumping
you on Q. But you and Q? I don't see that happening because fact
is he's got a man crush on Ceo. I mean, why else would he let the
guy walk all over him like he's a fucking doormat?"

"Are you finished?"

"Not quite. I'd like to put an offer out there. If you don't like
the sleeping arrangement, let me know. Ceo can sleep with Q, or
even under the stars, seeing as he's not worried about the bears."

After a beat, she says, "Thanks for the offer. Nature calls. Time
for you to go."

"All right. I just wanted you to know you have choices. But I can't
go back empty-handed. Stand behind me. I'm about to go lum-
berjack on this tree." Grahame shoulders past her, plants his feet,
raises the ax high over his head. Then arches his back and in one
smooth downward strike, chops through a branch the size of Ellie's
wrist. The ground shakes below her from the force of the blow.

Grahame picks up the branch, easily slings it over his shoulder.
He grins wide and says, "Da fire will be a blazin' soon, don't cha
know."

32

COLIN

Ceo says, "Q. What is wrong with you?"

"Nothing's wrong with me. Except I can't feel my big toes."

We're watching Grahame's light catch up to Ellie's.

He says, "You let that happen, dude."

"Let what happen?"

"*That.*" Nods at the two of them, now side by side, almost to the tree.

"Excuse me," I say, "for being a just a little confused. Are you saying I should have lunged for the ax before Grahame? Or that I should have tackled him after he grabbed the ax and wrestled it out of his Vulcan death grip?"

"Do I have to pick?"

"Tell me why this is my problem. She's your date, not mine."

They're at the boulder now. Two floating points of light in a sea of dark.

Ceo looks at me, shakes his head at the frustration of it all, then starts pulling his tent out of the stuff sack. He asks me to help him with the poles. I watch the dots of light a few seconds longer, then turn away, more than ready for something else to do.

A minute later we hear a sound that stops us both. Explosive, like a gunshot, and my first instinct is to run up the hill to check on Ellie. But Grahame is there, so what's the point of that? One of the lights starts bouncing down the hill. The other disappears behind the boulder. A minute after that Grahame walks into camp lugging a giant dead branch over his shoulder.

"See," he says to Ceo, tossing it down, "I told you the ax would come in handy."

33

COLIN

Dinner is macaroni and cheese with chunks of canned tuna topped with Ceo's answer to all seasonings: Tabasco sauce. He cooks it over a small camp stove that spits and sputters for ten minutes before it finally settles into a steady flame. Ceo claims it fired right up the last time he used it, then confesses it was four years ago on a sheltered beach in Mexico. Not who-knows-where on the side of a mountain at seven thousand feet with the temperature hovering at thirty degrees, and the wind freezing any part of the body that isn't covered in fleece or ten inches from a fire we had to keep small because of flying sparks. Ceo brought an extra ski hat which I'm wearing and the leather work gloves aren't keeping my fingers warm enough. My toes are the problem spot. I'm pretty sure that once the sun comes out and we're back on the trail, I'll be fine.

Another problem, and I'm not sure if I'd list it before or after bears, is the tent Grahame and I will be sleeping in tonight. Ceo bought it from a guy on Craigslist and didn't set it up before tonight. BIG mistake. The rain fly is too small and the grommets don't line up, so we can't stake it out. I'm not sure how much good it would be anyway because the waterproof lining is peeling like a bad sunburn. Since the stars are out in full force, we decide it isn't worth the trouble and leave it in the stuff sack. If the weather turns bad, we're out of luck, since Ceo's North Face tent is an ultra-lightweight that barely fits the two of them. He tried to pick up a weather forecast. No signal here for him either. Voilà! We are officially off the grid.

With the cold remnants of the macaroni and cheese forming a yellow cement in our aluminum plates and the fire reduced to yellow flickers over glowing coals, Ceo says, "Well, folks, I think it's time we head for the bags."

And there it is: the moment of truth.

The kick-in-the-gut moment I've been dreading ever since Ellie smiled at me at the overlook, and maybe even before that. Ellie hardly said a word during dinner, making me wonder what Grahame said to her and whether this moment is weighing on her, too. I need to know where her head is on all this. But getting to that information, given the way the stars are aligning, is an unknowable thing.

Then Ceo says, "But before we get all comfy we have some chores to do. Grahame, since you're the official bear sheriff, you get the honors of picking out the tree we'll use to hang the food. I'll keep you company. That leaves you two"—a nod to me and Ellie—"in charge of doing the dishes."

"I'm good with any plan that keeps me close to the heat," I say, resisting the urge to glance at Ellie.

Grahame says, "But I'm not. Since I'm the bear sheriff, I pick Ellie as my deputy."

Ceo says, "I think you'll like my original plan."

"Hard to see that happening."

"Do you remember when I told you I sold all the weed to buy the Laker tickets?"

"I'll never forget," Grahame says.

"Well, that isn't all true."

"How much isn't true?"

Ceo unzips a pocket in his coat. Waves a baggie with a couple joints inside.

Grahame smiles under his headlamp. If he was a dog, his tail would be wagging. He says, "Dude, let's hang some food."

Ceo says, "I figured you'd see the light. Colin, can you hand me the rope?"

It's on a rock next to their tent. We're about the same distance away, but I shrug and do as he asks. He meets me on the way back. As I hand it to him he whispers something in my ear.

Then he and Grahame walk into the woods.

One swinging a rope.

The other carrying an ax.

34

ELLIE

Colin scrapes the remains of dinner into the coals while Ellie pours water into the cooking pot, puts it on the stove, stands back to wait for the boil. Colin stands beside her, hands in the pockets of his jacket.

"Alone again, again," he says.

"Strange how that keeps happening." She remembers what Grahame said—*date-dumping*—and wonders if he's right.

They watch two headlamps move from tree to tree. She glances at the water. Bubbles are forming. Steam rises from the surface in feathery wisps carried away by the wind. She senses he has words in him, feels the tension of the unsaid by the way he stands stiff against the cold and shuffles his feet and keeps looking at her to see if she is looking at him. Well, she has words too. But time is working against them. The guys must have found a good tree because they are throwing a rock tied to a rope at a high branch. It shoots out like a spiderweb in the beams of their headlamps. The rock arcs over a branch on the second throw, and they lower it to the ground. As the stuff sack with their food rises up and up, Colin turns to her and says through a cloud of cold, "It's boiling."

"Oh." She uses her gloved hand to lift the pot off the stove. He holds out their plates, and she pours a little water in each. Their eyes catch and release. He swirls the sludgy water around, dumps it on the coals that hiss and steam. While he wipes the plates dry with a paper towel she looks out at the two guys and says, "I get the feeling that Grahame likes pot."

"He told me he wants twins just so he can name them Fattie and Blunt."

"And Ceo?"

"He's more on the retail end. His twins would be named Supply and Demand."

Ellie watches Colin stack the plates on a rock next to Ceo's pack. He returns to the fire and asks, "How did Ceo do it?"

"Do what?"

"Get you to say yes to a camping trip with three guys."

"Do you have a problem with it?"

"No. I'm glad you're here. Seriously glad, in fact. I'm just wondering how he did it."

She glares at Colin over the sparks. "You make it sound like it's all him. Like I didn't have a choice." As shock registers on his face, she adds, "Or maybe you think I'm some soccer slut looking for a romp in the woods with three racquet swingers."

"Hey, I'm sorry. That's not what I meant. If you'd—"

Ellie elbows him in the ribs. "Just kidding. I've been asking myself the same question." Ellie looks across the fire and into the woods. Ceo and Grahame are standing under the food sack hanging ten feet above their heads. They're passing something between them in the beam of their headlamp, smoke and vapor rising. She figures she has as much time as it takes them to share a joint. Back to staring at the flames, she says, "Ceo told me that he was coming with friends. He didn't tell me they were all guys. I assumed at least one would be a female. Or worst case, they'd all be female."

"So you had a surprise at the airport."

"Yes, I did. Two of them."

"You could have turned around."

"That's true. And I almost did."

"Yet here you are."

"Yet here I am."

"What stopped you?"

Laughter echoes down from the hill. Ellie recognizes the depth and tone. Grahame. She says, "How familiar are you with Newton's first law of motion?"

"I just happen to be taking physics this quarter. Objects at rest remain at rest; objects in motion remain in motion, unless acted upon by an outside force."

"That incomplete answer gets you a C-minus. An object at rest stays at rest, and an object in motion stays in motion at the *same speed* in the *same direction* unless acted upon by an unbalanced force."

"A C-minus is pretty harsh." Colin looks at her, smiling just a little. "So which are you? The object or the unbalanced force?"

Ceo starts howling like a wolf. Grahame joins him.

Colin says, "All right. So you're not the unbalanced force."

The wind shifts and picks up a little, blowing smoke in their faces. She waits for the smoke to clear, using the time to figure out how far she's willing to go. "My life has been moving in a straight line ever since I was ten. That's when people noticed that I was pretty good at kicking and catching a soccer ball. So those people made a plan. They said train hard. Hone my skills. Win tournaments. Make the Olympic Development Program. Train harder. Win more tournaments. Make the US national team. Win the Olympics. Get a gold medal. Make my family, town, and country proud."

"That's an impressive plan."

Ellie says nothing, waits to see if Colin will fill in the blanks.

He says, "But it isn't your plan."

"You raised your grade to a C-plus."

"That's all?"

"There's still room for improvement."

"You're worse than my mom. So tell me *your* plan."

"I'm taking next year off."

"Soccer or college?"

"Both."

Colin whistles between shivers. "That's bold. What are you going to do?"

Ceo tries to jump up and touch the food sack. Then Grahame tries. He falls. Ceo helps him up. Ceo tries and falls. They laugh, try again.

"I made a connection with a screenwriter at the workshop. I'm going to move into the apartment over her garage, get a job at a studio, and enroll in USC film school the following year. It's time to follow my deeply held passion."

161

"And that deeply held passion is...?"

After a beat, "Do you know how many females have received an Oscar for cinematography?"

"Please tell me there's at least one."

"Wrong. Eighty-nine shows, over six hundred fifty candidates. No woman has ever even received a *nomination*."

"That has to be among the worst shutouts in the history of shutouts."

"Someone has to end it."

"Someone with mad soccer skills, no doubt."

"It's my Olympic medal."

He nods while avoiding smoke. "And that's why she's quitting soccer."

"And you just raised your grade to an A-minus."

"Can't you do that after playing in the real Olympics?"

"My heart isn't there. It wouldn't be fair to the team."

"True that. Do your parents know about this plan?"

"No. But they will as soon as I get back."

"How will that go?"

"My father's still mad at me for skipping a showcase tournament to attend the workshop. When he hears my plan, his head will literally explode. My mom—she'll spend thirty minutes reminding me that she gave up her career as a pilot. That my little sister, Lizzy, didn't have a childhood, all so that I could follow my dream to be a professional soccer player. I'll tell her that it's been her dream, not mine. Then her head will explode, too."

"Is that a genetic condition, all these exploding heads?"

"The people of my tribe have very thin skulls. They're basically eggshells."

Grahame takes a final hit from the joint, tosses it to the ground, and grinds it with a boot. They start walking back to camp. It's a thirty-second journey. She watches Colin watch the fire, sees the gears turning.

The fire snaps. Sparks fly. He turns to her and says, "You met Ceo at the workshop."

"Correct."

"So you know his father owns Dancing Hippo Studios."

She smiles as Colin's eyes fill in the blanks.

"Congratulations, student Q. You earned an A-plus."

35

COLIN

We crawl into our respective nylon-walled bubbles, the zippers making a final closing statement on this night. Their tent glows orange under the stars. Ours smells like weed. I feel every bump and ridge of the rock beneath me, and the cold seeps up through my sleeping bag and into my skin, even though I'm wearing every piece of clothing I have. Grahame brought the ax. It is between us like a little fence. Once we're completely settled, Grahame turns off his headlamp. The other tent continues to glow. Thankfully my nightmare vision doesn't come true. There are no silhouettes, female shaped or otherwise.

Grahame asks, "Did you and Ellie have a nice little chat?"

"We did."

"Then can you explain how the hell she wound up with Ceo?"

I think about what she told me, and what I figured out. I could tell him the truth, that Ceo is a means to an end, but I don't see that being helpful in any possible way. That's a secret Grahame would not be able to keep. And it hurts me in ways I don't want to think about. All I say is, "He reminds her of Isaac Newton."

"The fig cookie dude?" Grahame laughs. Since he's way better at physics than I am, I figure that's the weed talking and say nothing.

A minute later he says, "She looks like a true athlete. Too bad she plays soccer. Can you imagine those legs in a tennis skirt? Man, I could watch her serve all day. Maybe I will."

I *hope* that's the weed talking.

The wind is picking up. After a few minutes of playing hockey with our tent, Grahame says, "Every time that happens I think it's a bear."

"Did you see *Kung Fu Panda*?"

"Yes."

"I pretend it's *that* bear."

The light goes off in the other tent.

Darkness descends to claim its long-awaited prize.

After a minute Grahame says, "Shit, Q. Do you need to move around so much?"

"I'm sorry. Are my chattering teeth keeping you awake?"

"Isn't camping awesome?"

"It's the best," I say.

An hour later Grahame is snoring while the wind roars over us like a thing unleashed. We are alone on the side of a mountain, where every creak and shudder traces back to padded feet with claws. My feet are cold. An ax blade keeps digging into my right shoulder. But none of that matters because my mind is looping the words Ceo whispered to me when I handed him the rope and Ellie stood by the fire, waiting.

This is your moment, Q. Use it or lose it.

* * *

Colin gets the text just as class is ending. Grahame wants to warm him up before his challenge match with Ceo, says to meet him on the glory court at three. Grahame usually warms up with some stud Coach brings in for him to play because Grahame is like a jungle cat and needs fresh meat. Colin usually warms up with Ceo and Rhody, but this offer from Grahame is too good, and this match and the scholarship that hangs in the balance is too important. Ceo will get what he needs. He always does.

Colin texts, OK, *while cutting through the library, where he hopes the kiosk girl with the short blond hair and nose ring will sell him a blueberry muffin. She is, she does. She tells him these muffins come from a bakery down by the pier and if he gets there before eight a.m. they'll still be warm. He tells her that sounds like an excellent way to start the day, but doesn't tell her that he would rather buy them from her even if they are cold and wrapped in plastic. She tells him, Oh, by the way. I'm there every Tuesday and Thursday at that time, gives him a smile and a napkin with his change. He puts one dollar in the tip cup and thinks about finally doing what he couldn't do last time or the time before that or the time before that.*

Ask her her name.

Ceo witnessed the most recent muffin-for-money-but-no-name moment and told him it was too painful to watch. He said, A, it's a good thing she doesn't sell lobsters, otherwise you'd be more broke than you are already, and B, there's no doubt she wants to trade bodily fluids with you, but dude, getting her name is like the base before first base. He then said, Observe, my friend, take notes if you must. He walked up to a random girl, said, Hi, my name is Ceo, what's yours?

Her name was Jilleine, spelled like caffeine, except with a Jill in front. Ceo had coffee with her the next morning. Which turned into yet another night sleeping off campus.

As he turns away she says, Bye, Colin.

He stops and smiles at her, and above the sudden pounding in his ears says, Thanks for the pastry, and oh, I'm wondering—

But the next guy in line steps between them, and she is occupied with another transaction. Colin walks away, muffin in hand, because that's how the world spins for people that say stupid shit like thanks for the pastry. Rather than dwell on the unrelenting order of his universe, he reminds himself that Grahame is waiting and he needs to get his head where it belongs:

On. The. Match.

He exits the library, and his phone rings.

Ceo.

Colin knows he shouldn't answer, but he does because otherwise he will never hear the end of it.

Hey, Colin says.

Where you at?

On my way.

Is there a muffin in your hand?

Yes.

And?

Blueberry.

No shit. And . . . ?

Colin sighs. She knew my name.

A laugh from Ceo. I guess you'll have to do the right thing and marry her.

You told her, didn't you?

We had a conversation about muffins and the people who buy them. I believe your name did come up. So did the word cute.

Colin responds by strangling the phone.

Ceo says, Did she give you a napkin with that muffin?

Yes.

Don't throw it away. That's all I'm saying. See you at warm-ups.

Ceo hangs up.

Colin looks at the napkin. She wrote in blue pen inside the fold: Emily 229-0037.

He throws away the muffin because eating a carb bomb right before a big match is a stupid thing to do. He had no intention of eating it anyway. He never does. But the napkin goes in his back pocket. He hates himself for putting it there.

Then he texts Ceo: Warming up with G. See you in 20 with my A game.

After the warm-up Grahame tells Colin to attack Ceo's backhand and his second serve. Make him bleed like a gutted hog when he hits the short ball, especially to your forehand, which you're hitting great. Don't be afraid to come to the net, just remember to cover the crosscourt pass when you do. That's his money shot. He'll spray down the line, nine out of ten. He may throw up a couple lobs, but they're more pathetic than his backhand. Play your game, Q, not his, an' eet will all be good, mon, don't cha know. Just don't let him fuck with your head. You won't let him do that, right?

Colin thinks about the homeless guy and the bird.

About the bet he lost and the pending trip to San Clemente.

About the napkin with the number he should call but now he won't.

About this match he can't afford to lose, because if he does, he drops out of the top two, and his scholarship goes down in flames.

Say it, Grahame repeats. Say you will not let him fuck with your head.

I won't let him fuck with my head, Colin says.

36
COLIN

I open my eyes, and the sky is gray. Someone is pouring water nearby. The sound resolves into Grahame bare-assed and pissing where the fire used to be. I sit up and smile because all is right with the world. Mother Nature shook us like Vegas dice all night long, and we're on the other side of it.

One night down, one to go.

Grahame pulls up, zips up.

I say, "So, we're not making a fire?"

He turns, sees me through the tent. "Dude, when nature calls, you don't put her on hold so you can dig a hole."

"But why on the fire rocks?"

"I needed something to aim at."

I unzip the tent, crawl out into the dawning day. I'm expecting a blast of cold but am happily surprised. The Vermonter in me guesses a temp around the freezing mark, maybe slightly above. The clouds are thick and drifting, like bored thugs looking for something bad to do. I scan full circle. There's a lot more rock than I remember from yesterday. Barren spots with drop-offs of uncertain height are scattered on a landscape featuring steep slopes and thinning trees. The mostly naked summits are clear of weather but not by much, including Mount Watkins, our destination for today. I give those clouds another suspicious look, then jam my fingers into my leather gloves, which are too much like me, stiff and cold. I hope we start for that summit sooner rather than later. But the other tent is zipped up tight with no visible signs of life therein.

Grahame asks, "How much sleep did you get?"

"A couple hours, maybe three. You?"

"More than that, but not much." He nods at the other tent, the one with a rain fly stretched tight as a drum. "So what do you think? Did he score or not?"

"I'm not going there," I say.

"Good thing we had that crazy wind."

"Why?"

"It drowned out all the other noises." He nudges me with an elbow.

I have zero interest in pursuing the meaning of *other*. The way he's looking at their tent, his eyes in a hooded squint, tells me where his mind is at, and I don't want to go there with him. Especially after what I learned last night.

"I need to dig a hole," I say.

"I need to make a fire."

He walks toward that giant branch, ax in hand.

I grab the TP and shovel and walk up the hill.

37

ELLIE

"**G**ood morning," he whispers, propped up on an elbow and smiling down at her. His tanned shoulders are bare. *When did that happen?*

"Back at you," she says.

"Sorry about my elbow last night."

"That's okay. I wasn't planning on using my spleen."

"Your hair looks amazing," he says.

"So does yours," Ellie says, pretty sure that Ceo is kidding about her hair, and she's dead serious about his. A stylist might spend an hour messing with his hair to get the same *tousled by a sleeping bag* look he's working to perfection right now.

Ellie pulls on her hat. Problem solved.

"What's that sound?" she asks.

"Grahame chopping wood."

"That man really likes to chop things."

"He seems to have a grudge against wood. I think his mother had sex with a beaver."

Ellie thinks about the force of Grahame's blow last night. How the ground shook, how the branch fell like a severed limb, and wonders how tennis balls survive the impact. "While we're on the subject of Grahame," she says, "how *did* you pass him on the trail?"

"I'd rather talk about beavers."

"You opened that door, not me. It's time to fess up."

He sighs in resignation. "My father is a bloodsucking corporate vampire. My mother is a ninja-warrior judge."

"So?"

"Do you know what that makes me?"

"A conflict of interest?"

"No," he says, frowning. "That sounds like something Q would say. I'm a *vampire ninja*. And nothing beats a vampire ninja."

"I see. While that's impressive, and probably true, I'll be more specific with my question. Grahame says you cheated. Did you?"

Ceo's eyes cloud for a moment. When they clear, the green is as hard as a gemstone. She considers withdrawing the question, but he says, "Vampire ninjas don't cheat. In fact we hate it more than anything. Our mission on this planet is to destroy cheaters and their cheating ways."

"Then how did you do it?"

"Vampire ninjas do not reveal their secrets. But for you I will make this one exception. Everything Grahame does is according to a plan. He's not capable of a random act. It works for him in tennis because he's so damn good he doesn't have to change his plan. But it kills him in poker because every hand is different. And he can't smell a bluff even if it's sitting on his face. That's how I passed his ass on the trail. Plus," he says with a shrug, "I talked him into putting a twenty-pound rock in his pack. I knew it would eventually take him down, and it did."

"Take him down? What does that mean?"

"I knew he wouldn't unpack all his shit to store the rock in the bottom of his pack. He put it on top. That made his center of gravity too high. He tripped and couldn't recover."

"So that's your story? He tripped?"

"Because of my genius plan. You sound disappointed."

"Would Grahame agree with your version?"

"Aw, I'm sure he thinks I tripped him. Truth is, I was hanging ten feet back, making sure he knew I was there. Just waiting for the inevitable. The only thing that tripped him was his ego."

Ellie thinks that when it comes to who has a bigger ego, Grahame or Ceo, it's basically a coin flip. Then considers a follow-up question, *Why didn't Colin go to San Clemente?* Or just as vexing, *Why didn't you see me when you were there?* She's trying to work out that segue when Ceo shines his eyes down on her and says, "So, Miss Ellie in the fetching ski hat. Let's move on to happier thoughts."

"Yes, let's."

"Are you ready for a day of wilderness adventure?"

"Why, of course."

He leans a little closer. Like he's thinking about doing something that doesn't involve talking. Lingers there for a moment, then reaches out with a finger, gently pushes her hat up an inch, and brushes her forehead with a soft, slow kiss. He pulls back a little, hovers, and for a startling moment she thinks he's going to work his way down. In that same moment she sees the weary eyes of the old cashier, and the box she chose not to buy. *Was that a mistake?* She licks her lips, suddenly aware that her sleeping bag feels warmer than it did a few seconds ago. But he pulls back all the way, slides her hat down as if covering the burning traces of what he did.

Ceo smiles at his work and waits.

"What?" she asks, trembling. His eyes don't leave hers.

"I need to get up."

"What's stopping you?"

"You're wearing my shirt."

Ellie groans, remembers when she woke up last night shivering. Ceo handed her something warm that smelled like sweat and woodsmoke. She put it on over her fleece sweater and fell asleep. *So that's how his shoulders got naked.* Ellie pulls off the shirt, hands it to him.

He sits up and puts on the shirt, showing a flash of the same rippled abs she has on her phone. And she remembers *I need to check my phone.*

He smiles at her. Again.

"Now what?" she asks.

"I, uh, need my pants."

This time she laughs.

"Is this what you models did in Montana?" she asks, feeling the warm rush of blood to her face.

"No. A hot tub was involved. Clothes were not."

Ellie wiggles inside her sleeping bag, gives Ceo his pants. "Please tell me that's everything."

"Let me check." He peers inside his bag. "Yup. That's all you got. You can turn or watch, I'm good either way."

Ellie faces the tent wall and thinks about the pounding in her chest, about what just happened and what didn't. Then she remembers last night. Where her thoughts were when she shivered in the dark and Ceo slept with his back to her. All she could see in that small space surrounded by wind was the look in Colin's eyes when he said, *Ceo's father owns Dancing Hippo Studios,* and again just before she followed Ceo to their tent. She saw wells of disappointment in those eyes, and wondered how deep they went. She wanted to tell him it isn't what he thinks. Yes, Ceo was the reason she came on the trip, but he isn't the reason she stayed. Unfortunately, she didn't have the time or opportunity for that talk, and even if she had, she doubted Colin would believe her.

Ellie notices the sound of chopping wood has stopped just before Ceo says, "It's safe to open your eyes."

She rolls onto her back, afraid to look up but unable to stop.

"Well, not completely safe," Ceo whispers while toying with the zipper on her sleeping bag. He leans down and down. She closes her eyes. His lips touch hers. His hand slides into her bag, touches her shoulder. Cold. She shivers.

Heavy footsteps approach their tent. They pause outside the door.

Grahame says, "Hey, chief, it's time to exit the love shack. We had a visitor last night."

Ceo says, "What kind of visitor?"

"The kind that shits in the woods."

"To be continued," Ceo whispers in her ear, and exits the tent.

It takes a full thirty seconds before Ellie can draw an easy breath.

She mouths, *Thank you.*

To Grahame.

38

COLIN

"**W**ell? Am I right?"

"Maybe," Ceo says to Grahame, who is poking one of four meatball-size mystery turds with a stick. They're deposited as if making a statement, directly under the branch where they hung the food last night. The droppings are still a little moist, even in the near-freezing air. We didn't find any paw prints, but that could be because the ground is too hard. I look down at Ceo's tent. No sign of Ellie.

"*Maybe?*" Grahame says. "What else could it be?"

"A deer. A badger. Lots of forest animals could do this."

"We're not being stalked by a fucking badger."

Sensing the tension in Grahame's voice and hoping to keep things light, I say, "It could be Sasquatch's cousin, Assquatch. He's known for this kind of shenanigans."

Ceo smiles. Grahame spears a turd.

"Q could be right," Ceo says, stroking his chin. "Or we could have a more serious problem."

"Like what?" Grahame says.

"There's a sleep shitter among us."

This earns a questioning look from me and Grahame.

"Some people walk in their sleep," Ceo explains. "Sleep shitters have the same problem except with a twist. They take dumps in very strange places. Usually the family pet gets blamed. Or"—he gives Grahame a sideways glance—"in this case, badgers."

"Do sleep shitters do this?" Grahame asks, and points to the fresh marks on the tree where bark had been scraped off. They go up about fifteen feet, stopping just below the branch that had supported the stuff sack.

"If they're crazy enough," Ceo says. "Maybe you should check your nails for bark chips."

Grahame is six feet from Ceo. Steam billows from his nose like an angry bull into a sky that matches his mood—considerably darker than it was ten minutes ago. After a beat he says, "Maybe if you weren't so busy doing your thing last night, we wouldn't have this problem."

"And what *thing* is that?" Ceo says, his voice flat.

"It shouldn't be too hard to figure out, *chief*," Grahame says, smiling at Ceo. "Seeing as you only have one move." He uses the stick to flick a turd at Ceo. It misses, but not by much.

Ceo takes a step toward Grahame. I slide between the two of them, arms out, saying, "I think we've all talked enough shit for today."

For a long moment I feel like I'm on a track between two runaway trains. Then Grahame nods slowly, turns, and heads for camp. That's when I notice Ellie is up. She's facing us while stuffing her sleeping bag into a sack. We watch in silence as Grahame walks right up to her, wraps his arms around her, and gives her a big hug.

Ellie's feet kick helplessly at the ground. It goes on for several seconds before he finally lets go. It looks like Ellie may have pushed him, but it's hard to tell from here.

"You and me," Ceo says. "We need to talk."

39
ELLIE

"Good morning, sunshine," Grahame says, heading straight for her like a bullet.

Something in his voice doesn't sound right. There's a darker intent behind his smile, and she sees it sparking in his eyes. Colin and Ceo are still by that tree. She wishes they weren't.

"Good morning," Ellie says. "What were you guys—"

Grahame slams into her, wraps his arms around, and pulls tight. She feels the crushing knot of his biceps under his jacket as her feet leave the ground, is thankful for the sleeping bag acting as a buffer between her and the pressing parts of him. She works a hand free, uses it to push back against his chest. It's like trying to move a wall of stone.

"Let...me...go," she gasps.

He puts her down, relaxes his arms. Then steps back and says, "Thanks, Ellie. I feel better now." That thing she saw sparking in his eyes is gone. They are as cold and gray as the unflinching sky. Of all the voices calling for attention in her head, there is only one that demands immediate action. It has been there since the beginning of it all, and she's been ignoring it for far too long.

It's time for this camping trip to end.

40

COLIN

Ceo agrees with Ellie's logic. It's hard not to. Since we can't get a forecast and the clouds have dropped so low that they're covering some of the higher peaks, we decide it's time to bail and head for home. But Mount Watkins is still clear, and Ceo suggests that since we're this close, *this close*, we may as well bag at least one summit.

"How long will that take?" Grahame asks.

"It's only a couple miles." Ceo checks his watch. "It's eight forty now. We'll be on top before eleven, have a quick lunch, then work our way down to the trail. I bet we'll be in the valley before dark and in LA by midnight."

Ellie says, "My flight leaves at six."

"We'll have you in Fresno by four."

"What if it rains?"

"Anything more than a drizzle and we turn around."

"Could it snow?" I ask.

"Doubt it. The temperature is going up. We'll be down before it gets cold enough." Then he says into our collective silence, "Hey, if the weather turns, we bail."

Mount Watkins sounds reasonable, his precautions make sense. I'm not so sure about his call on the snow. I've been skiing enough to know that it can be raining at the base and whiteout conditions at the top. And we're talking about heading up before we head down. On the other hand, we're dealing with the Ceo Effect, and that can't be ignored.

We all nod in agreement.

"Okay," he says. "Let's go see Mr. Watkins."

Ceo skips practice to give Colin a ride to the airport, but not without a beach stop first. Says there's no way I'm letting you fly to cow country without a serious dose of wave therapy. Colin agrees as long as they leave by eight. That gives him a two-hour buffer for the drive to LAX, to pass through security, then catch the 10:50 red-eye to Burlington for an 8:35 a.m. arrival. He's not sure who will pick him up because his mother wasn't thinking or talking clearly. The $1,200 airfare drained the emergency Visa, so renting a car is not an option.

Ceo doesn't ask what happened to his dad. Colin doesn't offer. Instead he tells Colin that his Q-tip video on YouTube has already passed the blind kid throwing knives at his drunk uncle and the dog that runs in circles every time it sees a squirrel, and it almost has as many views as the penguin that deals blackjack with its beak. He says, Dude, that's freaking awesome for only half a day. Ceo drops the subject because Colin just stares at his phone, and his silence is thicker than the five o'clock traffic on the PCH.

They start out tossing the Frisbee, then switch to football. Doing hero catches into the waves up and down the beach. The water is shockingly cold, but the air is warm enough. Colin feels himself breathing again after too many hours of not being sure it was worth the effort. Facing a classic SoCal sunset that Ceo rates a solid 7.2, they sit down without towels on the sand and let nature do the drying. After a couple of minutes of watching the waves fill in footprints and crumble sand castles and make things smooth for the next day, Ceo asks Colin what happened.

He died, Colin says.

How?

Mom didn't say.

What did she say?

That he's dead and can I come home.

Just that?

No. She cried these deep gasping sobs that tore me up inside. It's like I didn't know who was on the other end. I listened to that until she finally said, Colin I can't do this, just come home. And ended the call. I tried reaching her after class, but the line was busy.

Did you text her?

She doesn't text.

Dude, I can't believe you went to class. With a Q-tip in your ear hole.

I had a final, Ceo. I didn't know what else to do.

Well, first thing is you pull out the Q-tip.

So simple, yet so wise. Then what?

You don't take the final.

And risk losing what's left of my financial aid?

They would've made an exception. Your freaking father died.

Colin watches the waves roll in.

Ceo punches him in the shoulder. I had to hear the news from Coach.

I know. I'm sorry.

My travel agent would have found you a better flight than that shitty red-eye. You'd be home by now.

I couldn't afford a better flight.

We could've worked something out.

Colin doesn't say he thought about calling him and knew he would step up. He's that kind of friend and would never ask for it back. But by then he was numb and the tailspin was in motion and somehow he turned left and right and walked down some stairs and wound up in class.

Ceo says, It's okay, Q-tip. But next time your dad dies, call me first.

I'll do that, Colin says, and feels the beginning of a smile. He wonders if that name will stick, hopes this is the end of it. After a minute he says I'm going to need a rental car when I get there.

Ceo laughs, says, I can make that call. Then checks his watch.

Dude, it's seven fifty-five. We should head.

Colin stands barefoot behind the Mercedes, waiting for the trunk to pop so he can get to his phone and see if his mom called. Maybe change out of these clothes so he doesn't have to fly across the country with sand in his crotch. But the trunk isn't opening and isn't opening and then Ceo looks at him with oh-shit in his eyes.

Says, I forgot there's a hole in the pocket of these damn shorts.

A hole? What are you telling me?

Dude, the key. It's, like, fucking gone.

41

COLIN

Ellie is twenty yards ahead of me.

She's following Grahame, who is thirty yards behind Ceo, who is not following any discernible trail and hasn't been since late yesterday afternoon. He's traversing upward, carving random switchbacks through low bushes and over granite slabs. The increasingly steep terrain will soon become all granite because the summit, from what we've seen of it, is one massive dome of barren rock. Meanwhile the clouds get closer, the air colder, and there's a bear in our rearview mirror. All this is feeding an unkillable notion that we're being squeezed from every side and going up before we go down is a deeply flawed concept.

What I'm trying not to think about is how she hasn't spoken a word to me this morning. No, I take that back. After we finished packing up our gear, she handed me the remains of her Pop-Tart and said, *Could you finish this for me?* This coming at the tail end of a chain of events that led to the decision (initiated by her) to leave today. The two biggest links in that chain being whatever happened last night in Ceo's tent, and that bear hug stunt Grahame pulled this morning while Ceo and I watched like idiots. Which gets me thinking. Maybe I'm a link in that chain. Maybe Ellie regrets telling me the truth about why she's on this trip, and even worse, thinks I told Grahame and now she blames me for what he did.

Then there's Ceo telling me we need to talk. No shit about that. But he's up there and I'm back here, so how's that going to work? This whole mess is a second-guessing parade, and I'm in the middle of it. I glance up, and Ellie has stopped at the edge of a long patch of granite. Oblivious, Grahame and Ceo keep walking. She watches me as I close the distance between us, then stop a few feet from her, panting vapor in the thin, cold air.

Ellie says, "Not that this is any of your business, which it isn't. I'm sure you think something happened last night in the tent. That I sealed the deal, or whatever you male types like to say. Well, you're wrong, *bucko.*" Then she turns and says as she walks away, "So you can be finished not talking to me."

42

ELLIE

Ellie smiles to herself, thinking about the stunned look on his face. His jaw hanging open, eyes wide. It was perfect and what she hoped for. Counts to seven before hearing him say, "Wait a minute! You can't throw that pitch and walk off the mound."

"Sorry. I have a rule—no sports metaphors. *Ever.* Try again, please."

After a beat, "You said I think something happened and that I'm wrong."

"Correct."

"So what you really said is *nothing* happened."

"Correct."

"But nothing is, in fact, something."

She smiles to herself again. "I'll allow that."

"So now I'm wondering how she feels about nothing."

"She feels very good about nothing."

The voice behind her is silent. Ceo and Grahame have disappeared over a ridge.

Then Colin says, "What if...?"

"Yes?"

"What if it was someone else in the tent?"

"Would that someone else have holes in his sneakers?"

"He would buy new sneakers for the occasion."

Ellie stops so he can catch up. She wants Colin to see the smile in her eyes when she says, "Now *that* would be something."

43

COLIN

The summit ridge is a broad and barren place dotted with oddly shaped rocks, some as round and smooth as giant eggs, with clusters of tough old trees scattered about. As we search for Ceo and Grahame my thoughts should be on how we're finally at the top of this thing and are about to turn around. I should be focused on those clouds and how that heavy bucket is about to tip. But instead my thoughts are trained like lasers on the person standing so close that I can smell the chocolate on her breath, drilling into this single unbelievable fact that she is choosing me over Ceo. I smile and repeat it to myself, as if the act will make it more real.

Me. Over. Ceo.

Statistically it's in the same ballpark as a one-armed monkey performing face-transplant surgery. But I'm allowing myself to go there. To believe this one big thing despite the fact that she could be playing me like she's playing Ceo. Although those odds are less than monkey transplant surgery because with me there's nothing to play. Ceo can promise her rippled abs, baby models, and studio connections that help fulfill her deepest-held passion. I can promise her a lifetime supply of maple syrup and fresh bass. It's not what I or any sane person would define as a close call.

But I refuse to snuff out this fragile flame of hope.

Which leads to the question of how this development will play out on planet Ceo. He obviously trusts me with her. Otherwise why would he put me in so many situations where we are alone? On the other hand, why not trust some kid from Vermont who doesn't have the nerve to ask a girl selling muffins if she has a name?

Then there's his whispered comment to me last night, *This is your moment, Q. Use it or lose it.* It confused me then, and continues to bounce around in my brain like an evil echo. Earlier this morning, just after Grahame pulled his stunt, Ceo said we need to talk. That's a lot of cryptic shit he's flinging my way, even for him. Now there's a ripple in the status quo that puts things spinning in a whole new direction. I may have to force the issue and have that talk, tell him that trusting me may not be the best card in his hand.

I follow Ellie up a well-defined trail on the rock, pass a bow-shaped tree along the way. It leans heavily to one side and looks like it was bent in a hurricane. I ask her to take a couple pictures for my mother, one of me inside the bow with Half Dome framed in the distance, and one with me just looking off into space. She shows me the shots on her camera. They're amazing. Even in the small viewing screen I can tell she has talent. Then, while we're still close and with those brown eyes going deep, she asks me how my father passed. For once I'm able to answer that question without deflecting, as if I can see beyond the hurt.

"My mom was upstairs watching *Jeopardy!* reruns and making lunch for Dad. Sliced radishes with Vermont cheddar and fresh dill on pumpernickel. He was in the basement tying flies for a fishing trip with a friend that afternoon. Mom called down to let him know that his lunch was ready. He didn't answer. She called again. He didn't answer. She found him on the floor, eyes wide open like a mounted fish. She knew in that instant that he was gone."

"A heart attack?"

"Massive aneurysm. He died in seconds."

"Colin, that's awful. I'm so sorry."

"He died with feathers glued to his fingers and a fishing hook in his hand. That's how he'd want to go."

"Was...was that the Q-tip morning?"

I nod. "Definitely not the way I wanted to burn my fifteen minutes of fame."

"Thanks for telling me."

"Thanks for asking. I've never told anyone about the radish sandwich. Not even Ceo."

She smiles, leans forward, and kisses my cheek. Time literally stops. The bear, the clouds, all the baggage of this day fades to nothing while I consider kissing her back because I think she wants me to, so I face her and—

A familiar voice shouts from above, "Hey, kids!"

We turn to see Ceo waving from what better be the top of this mountain, since there's nothing beyond him except air.

A short walk later we're shrugging off our packs next to Ceo's, with him saying, "Welcome to the top of Bruce Willis's head, also known as the summit of Mount Watkins." I look around quickly. There is no sign of Grahame or his pack. Ceo leads us down a short distance on the valley side to the edge of the void. In front and to the left are thousand-foot death plunges leading to the valley floor, which is nearly clear of smoke. To the right, on this side of the valley, is a steep granite slope leading down to yet another vertical wall. Across the void, the very top of Half Dome is capped by clouds. Ceo points to and names some of the surrounding geography that is still visible, while Ellie's camera clicks. Clouds Rest is particularly interesting, with its broad gray flank and odd shapes and depressions. It looks like the hide of some ancient, wrinkled beast.

When Ceo is finished, I ask him, "Where's Mount Grahame?"

"Skulking around here somewhere."

I scan the summit. There aren't that many places to hide.

I ask, "Why is he skulking?"

"We were having a chat about a thing—"

"A thing?"

"Yeah. A thing. Then he goes all Jamaican pimp on me, and you know how I feel about that. I asked him to stop, but he kept on going. So I told him he violated the terms of our no-accent deal, and I did what I had to do."

"What did you probably not have to do?"

"I Bic'd the other half of the hundred."

"You *burned* it?"

"I knew I'd never get his half back. So, yeah."

"And now he's pissed."

A shrug and a half smile from Ceo. "Just a wee bit, mon."

I know from poker that Grahame often talks in that accent when he's stressed. It's the most obvious tell in the history of the game. Something had to be the cause of that effect.

"What was the *thing* you talked about?"

"That's between me and the pimp."

He gives me a quick look like maybe it isn't.

Ellie's camera continues to click, but there was a definite pause.

Since Grahame still has his pack, I ask, "Is he coming back?"

A shrug from Ceo says he doesn't know, doesn't care. He reaches into his pants pocket and comes out with the GPS. He says, "Ellie? Do you mind if I take a short walk with Q? I need his help calibrating this thing."

She asks with the camera swinging from Ceo to me, "How many men does it take to calibrate a GPS?" *Click, click, click.*

"Five," Ceo says. "But two Smurfs with skills can manage."

"What's wrong with it?" *Click, click, click, click.*

"It says we're at sixty-two hundred feet. I know we're around eight."

Ellie lowers the camera. "You said it was working yesterday."

"True. That was before this morning. Since then it fell out of my pack and bounced off a couple rocks. Now it just keeps searching." He shows her the face of it.

"You've rebooted?"

"Twice."

"Well," she says, looking at the two of us, "I guess you'd better get started."

I think about Grahame. About the odds of him returning while we're gone versus the odds of him not returning at all. Neither option works for me. But I know this isn't about the GPS. And I suspect Ellie does, too.

"You're okay with this?" I ask.

"Oh, sure. That gives me some quiet time with Mr. Willis's head." Ellie plants herself on a rock facing the void. Takes the remains of a chocolate bar out of her pocket and snaps off a chunk. Waves at our hesitation, saying, "Go already. Go forth and calibrate."

We start walking, get about twenty feet when Ellie says, "Hey, guys? Did you feel that?"

"Feel what?" I ask.

"A raindrop."

We wait thirty seconds. In that short span the wind dies to a mere whisper. That takes the sting out of the air. But I don't trust this sudden calm. It's like we're floating on a raft in a slow-motion current with the uneasy rumble of something big around the bend. Meanwhile the clouds continue to drift and morph and hang so low I swear I can hear them oozing over the rocks.

"Guess I was wrong," Ellie says.

"We'll be back in ten minutes," Ceo tells her.

"Make it nine."

Colin is in bed on top of the covers, staring at the ceiling tiles, listening to the muted thumping of music down the hall and the constant background hum of traffic and sirens somewhere outside his window while

Grahame watches a movie on his laptop in the dark with headphones on. He prefers all this to the catfight in his head every time he closes his eyes. That's when he replays his conversation with Ceo after the match and it Just. Won't. Stop.

Ceo pulling up to him while he stood at some crosswalk, miles from where he should be, waiting for the light to change.

He said, C'mon, Q. You're being crazy. Get in.

Colin said, I need to walk.

Ceo said, Maybe, but not here. Don't be a crime statistic. I'll buy you dinner. We'll work this out.

Colin said, I've been mugged once today. It can't get any worse.

Ceo said, I gave you clemency anyway. That should be worth something.

Colin didn't answer.

The light changed.

Ceo yelled over the traffic and horns behind him, I'm sorry, Colin.

And drove away.

He wonders if sleep will ever come. Or if this day will turn into the next without changing one molecule of its structure. He wonders about Coach, about the disappointment in his eyes when he saw the score of the third set, 6–0. Wonders if that disappointment will still be there when the new day finally comes and Coach has to tell him that he lost his scholarship.

And his phone buzzes.

CEO

Can't sleep. You?

COLIN

No.

CEO

Still pissed?

Yes.

The phone goes dark. Colin hopes that's the end of it. Considers turning off his phone, or putting it in a drawer under his socks. But his mother might call, and those events he can never miss. So he keeps the phone in its sacred spot, beside his bed on top of Robert Frost.

Five minutes later the phone buzzes again.

Still pissed?

Still yes. WTF??!

San Clemente?

He types, Not interested.
DELETE.
He types, No Way!
DELETE.
He types, No. Freaking. Way.
DELETE.
Shakes his head.
Types

COLIN

FUCK San Clemente.

SEND.

44
ELLIE

Ellie watches them hike up to the summit. Smiles as the GPS finds its way back into Ceo's pocket. She returns her gaze to the valley, nibbles on her chocolate while considering the unlikely progression of today. It started in Ceo's tent, waking up next to him. When he smiled down at her, there was something in his eyes, the hint of a more-than-casual interest that she'd been looking for ever since that walk on the beach in Santa Cruz. She didn't see it at the airport, in the car, or basically anywhere on the trail, since his attention has been focused on a chest-thumping match with Grahame. She figured somewhere between the text he sent and their embrace at the Fresno airport, he'd found a shiny new object more aligned with his model-world tastes.

And then this morning happened. He kissed her. She held her breath while he tugged the zipper on her sleeping bag, teased it down one click at a time. But he left moments later to pursue yet another thing with Grahame. And she could breathe again. *Well, none of that matters now.* It's ancient history, like this valley spread out before her. Last night, in the ten minutes it took Ceo and Grahame to share a joint, she revealed secrets to Colin about her future plans that even Nadia didn't know. She was certain that deeper moment of truth would cause him to think less of her. He'd see that when it comes to collecting shiny objects, she's in the same orbit as Ceo.

Then the big surprise later this morning. The Great Wall of Colin cracked and he opened up just enough for her to see some light. Ellie smiles at this unexpected development while contemplating these three undeniable truths. Ceo looks amazing catching a Frisbee. His father owns a movie studio. But Colin quotes John Cusack, and that quality alone offers an entire universe of unexplored potential.

She finishes off her chocolate, feels another raindrop hit her cheek. A shiver runs through her even though there is no wind, senses a deeper chill and wonders about the source. *Shouldn't they be back by now?* She turns around just in time to witness a wall of gray crawl over and engulf the summit dome. The horizon east and west are gone, the surrounding rocks and trees reduced to dissolving shadows. Seconds later the cold wraps around her. It is thick and wet, and the rocks it touches are coated with a shiny glaze.

She scans her world and gasps.

There is no valley.

No Half Dome.

No sky.

Ellie is ten yards from a vertical wall that plunges down for a thousand feet. But she doesn't know where it is. All she sees in every direction is gray.

45

COLIN

We hike up to the summit dome, do a quick scan for Grahame, and come up empty. Ceo says this isn't far enough, so we walk a couple hundred yards down to a cluster of trees and rocks overlooking Clouds Rest. I'm uncomfortable being this far away from Ellie. We could have stayed at the summit next to the packs and had all the privacy we needed. But this is Ceo's play, and he walked this far for a reason. It clearly has nothing to do with the GPS unless he plans on calibrating it from the inside of his pocket. I'm wondering how I can bring up Ellie and her revelation this morning, or maybe not bring it up at all because hell, we're leaving today, so what's the point? That's when Ceo turns to me, and the first words out of his mouth since we left Ellie are, "Dude, I seriously fucked up."

I assume he's talking about whatever that *thing* is he said to Grahame that sent him into his latest snit. If his absence continues much longer, with the weather looming like it is, this situation will escalate from minor irritation to *serious issue*.

I say, "How bad?"

"Kittens in a blender bad."

"Whoa. That's a serious kinda bad."

"More than you know."

"I know burning the hundred was not cool."

"Nah, he deserved it. The part I'm talking about was before that."

"Is it because you sold the weed?"

"That contributed. But more before than that."

"How much before?"

"You remember our last poker game?" He picks up a rock, hurls it over the edge. It sinks down into a gray soup that has consumed Clouds Rest and the valley below. I know it is creeping our way, that the landscape is fading before our eyes.

"Yeah," I say. "It's the game you duped us into Cannabis Cove."

"There was no duping involved. Anyway, I'm talking *before* that."

Before the poker game gets into darker times. He could be talking about the challenge match and the cascading storm of shit that followed. I don't see how or why. I've been moving past those days, and I thought he was, too. Maybe I'm wrong.

"So this is about me?"

"You and me," he says, throwing another rock. "And Ellie."

My body stiffens. It's as if he threw that rock at my gut.

"What about her?"

"The kittens are in the blender, Q. If I tell you, that means I'm pushing the button."

"Push away."

"All right," and he fixes his gaze on a distance we can no longer see. "A couple months ago I was at this thing, and I met a girl."

"Here you go with this thing again. What is it this time?"

"Not important. Anyway, I met a girl. I wasn't into her then, at least not a lot. But I thought she might be a good fit for a good friend, so the more I got to know her, the more I thought, yeah, she would be a good fit for this friend. But as luck would have it, this friend was on the other side of the country, so I couldn't do much about it."

Ceo pauses. I feel him looking at me, as if I might have words to say.

I do. But I choose different words. "Go on."

He says, "So the friend returns from that state. I still want him to meet this perfect-match girl, so I look her up on the Internet, and as luck would have it, she's going to be at a different event in another town not too far away. I know my friend will never meet her on his own and he's too stubborn to be set up. So I create a reason to go to that town and invite him along."

Another pause.

I fill it. "The event is a soccer tournament. And the town is San Clemente."

"Good. You know the friend I'm talking about. It takes some convincing plus a little help from a seagull and a sandwich, but he says yes. I'm thinking this will be so freaking sweet. They'll get married, have babies, name the first one Ceo, and we'll be friends forever. But unfortunately on that very same day we have a mishap. I do something stupid, lose my shit at a challenge match, and that night he sends me a three-word text."

"'Fuck San Clemente.'"

"Very un-Colin."

I take a deep breath. The cloud has reached us now. It's so thick and cold it hurts my lungs. But the pain actually feels good. It distracts from the other pain.

Ceo says, "Now, more than ever, I want my friend to meet this girl. I know he'd rather light his hair on fire than let me hook him up, especially since the mishap. But desperate times, desperate measures, right? So I go to plan B. I put this whole camping trip together thinking that if I pull this off, man, I can undo that mishap and make things right."

Mishap?

Make things right?

It takes a moment for the crushing weight of this news to hit. When it does, I nearly buckle from the impact. I say through clenched teeth, "Define *whole trip*."

He starts talking, and I feel rage boiling up as numbness sinks in. He says he knew I wouldn't go on the trip if it was just him and me and Ellie. He came up with the Cannabis Cove idea, knowing that would guarantee buy-ins from Grahame and Rhody. Then he actually paid Rhody fifty bucks to back out of the trip to make room for Ellie. Rhody was all over that because he was a little nervous about Coach finding out. Ceo says he chose Cannabis Cove because he knows if he was getting high with Grahame, I would have plenty of bonding time with Ellie. But Cannabis Cove went up in smoke. Then he picked the Snow Creek Trail and talked Grahame into a *race that nearly killed us both by the way*, so I could have that private time with Ellie. When he's finally done, he says, "So there you have it, kittens in a blender."

There's movement a little to my left and behind me. A shadow shifting in the gray. I take a quick glance, but the fog is so thick that I can't see beyond the next rock. I refocus on Ceo, thinking we need to get back to Ellie. But he's rolling now, and I'm in too deep to make him stop.

I ask, "Did Grahame know about any of this?"

"Negative. Just Rhody."

"Does he know now?"

"I don't think so."

"You don't *think*?"

"That's where we had our recent problem. He started telling me how he was going to give Ellie some free tennis lessons, take her out, see if he can score. I told him that wasn't going to happen in this lifetime, or the next three after that. He said what the hell do you care, you haven't spent a single minute alone with her other than last night. Then he said *an dat puts her een da fookin' play, chief, don't cha know.* That's what led to me burning the Benjamin. Freaking dumb-ass Bob Marley wannabe from freaking Minnesota."

This is way beyond what I can take. Grahame thinks he's free to make moves on Ellie. He's pissed at Ceo even more than normal, and now he's gone rogue. Ellie has no idea about any of this. I replay the hug he gave her this morning, his massive arms trapping her, lifting her off her feet like a toy. I say, "I've heard enough. We need to get back," and start to turn.

He grabs my arm. "Not yet, Q. The kittens are in the blender. But I haven't pushed the button."

I freeze. However far I thought we had gone down this road, he's about to go further.

"What else is there?" I say.

"I've been keeping my distance from Ellie. It's been hard, but that's what I did. You remember back at the overlook when that lady was taking a picture, and I switched places? That was me putting her next to you. Then I left you alone at the fire last night. I gave you all the opportunities I could to make it work." He trails off, leaving *make it work* out there like a bomb with a burning fuse. "Since you didn't take advantage, I let her in, man. I let her in. Now the thing is ... I don't want her out."

"Take *advantage*? Are you serious?"

"You know I am."

"Like, here's my queen, you can take her with your *knight*?"

"I don't play chess."

"Bullshit. You do it with people. All the fucking time."

He looks at me, his eyes narrowing.

"She's a real person, Ceo. She's not a commodity. Not a prize, not a trophy. She's not something you trade or give away."

"I know. I know. The problem is I'm falling for her. Hard. Something happened in the tent this morning."

Something happened? It's like he knocked me down and stepped on my throat. I'm shaking. What little control I have is slipping away. I start to back up, to get out of arm's reach, afraid of what I might do.

Ceo says, "I'm sorry, Q."

"You're sorry? Like you were sorry after the match?"

"It was the truth then. And it's the truth now."

"Your truth is like this fucking fog. I can see it, smell it. But when

I try to actually hold on to it—*POOF!* Nothing's there!" I realize that I'm yelling. I take a breath, lower my voice. "So stop saying the *S* word, okay? I don't want to hear it."

He stares at me. Then his eyes go wide. "Holy shit! You're into her."

I just stand there, motionless in the fog.

"Tell me I'm wrong, Q. Tell me you're not."

"I . . . I can't do that."

He smiles, shakes his head. "Dude, I told you they were in the blender."

"Yeah. At least that much was the truth."

"So now what?"

"You have to tell her. Everything."

"I'll do it at the airport."

"Sooner."

"All right. On the switchbacks going down. What about Grahame?"

"You've got him spun up enough already. If he finds out that you played him just to set me up with Ellie . . ." I shake my head at the grim prospects of that revelation. "You'd be better off facing the bear."

"Nah, I can handle him. But hopefully, he's already on his way down, because if he touches her—"

From over the summit and out of the fog.

Ellie screams.

46

COLIN

We turn to run—and can't. Visibility is down to less than thirty feet. We stayed too long. Shit. I take two steps, slip, and fall to the ground. The rock against my hands, even through the gloves, is cold and dark and smoother than it looks. The fog is starting to freeze. Ceo's hiking boots have better traction than my worthless sneakers. I tell him I'm all right, GO! GO! GO!

He takes off like a shot and disappears in a swirl of gray. I struggle to my feet and start walking in what feels like a straight line, hoping to intersect the trail leading to the summit. I figure as long as I keep moving up, I'll be all right. Ellie only screamed once. She hasn't answered any of Ceo's calls, and I haven't heard anything from him for at least a minute. The fear of getting lost in this soup and walking off a cliff is real and paralyzing.

I come to a spot with a distinctive white seam in the granite that I remember being just below the summit. I turn a few degrees to the left and continue moving up. Another fifty feet in that direction and I see dark shapes on the ground that resolve into our packs. By the time I reach them I hear voices from below, moving toward me.

One of them says, "The hell have you been?"

The other says, "Ah been lost in dee clouds, mon."

The third says, "Next time you do that to me I'll stab you in the eye with my spork."

We take a few minutes to debate our options. It's a short list. We can hike down now or wait for the cloud to move. The problem is we don't know if this is an isolated cloud or a blanket. A little wind would help. The air is so still that when Ceo drops a couple pine needles, they fall straight to the ground. Not much chance of the cloud moving in these conditions. Grahame says the risk of the ice getting worse isn't as bad as the fear of becoming lost and doing an accidental cliff dive. He says it almost happened to him twice already.

Ceo argues that this is one of the easiest descents off a mountain ever and that we should head down now before the ice gets worse. That if we can just get a little lower maybe we'll be out of this shit and can reach the valley before the weather turns. He reminds us that if the weather does turn, this shelterless summit will make last night's storm look like a blow-dryer on an elephant's ass. That isn't enough to convince the rest of us, especially Ellie. She's still shaking from whatever happened while we were gone. Combine that with the two falls I took getting to this point, and I'm all over the sit-and-wait option. Give it an hour and reevaluate.

The vote is three to one.

We sit on our packs and wait.

Ellie helps distract us from the cold seeping through and in by describing what happened. How when the cloud showed up she became disoriented and was afraid to move. She says that kind of thing had never happened to her before. That she knew which way to go, which way the summit was, but without a horizon and the cliffs so close, it's like the world in her head just disappeared and no matter which way she went it would send her tumbling down and down and down.

"So I stood there," she says, "shivering, getting more and more disoriented, waiting for you guys to come back. But you didn't come back." Ellie looks at me and Ceo, eyes flaring under her hat.

"Sorry we took so long," I say.

"We weren't paying attention," Ceo says. "It snuck up on us."

"Did you finish your calibrating at least?" Ellie asks.

I look at my hands.

"We got a good start," Ceo says. "But I think it's still broken."

Grahame leans in, saying, "What's this about calibrating?"

"Let me finish my story first," Ellie says. "I'm getting to the best part. So anyway, there I am, alone in a death cloud. Then I hear a sound, a kind of grunt off to my right—"

"Which was me nearly falling on my ass," Grahame says.

"So I turn to see what it is—and this huge bear-shaped thing emerges out of the mist. I can't run. I'm afraid to move. So I yell at it."

"Which scared the holy crap out of me," Grahame says.

"Well, don't sneak up on people when there are bears about!"

"How can I sneak up on something that I can't see?"

"If I can see you, then you can see me."

There's a little heat to those words. It silences Grahame, but only for a moment. Then he nods to her and says, "Tell them about the rock."

"I picked up a rock and threw it."

"Meanwhile," Grahame says, "this alleged bear-shaped thing that happens to walk on two feet, carry a backpack, and speak *English* is telling her to calm down, it's just me. And she hits me with a freaking rock." He rubs his shoulder. "Goalie girl's got an arm on her. I bet there's a bruise."

"That was an impressive throw," I say to Ellie.

"Not really. I was aiming at his head."

Ceo says, "In that case, your throw sucked. Because I'm wondering how you could miss a target that big."

"And I'm wondering," Grahame says, leveling his eyes at Ceo, "why you left Ellie as bear bait."

After a beat, "We were calibrating the GPS."

"What's wrong with it?"

"It's hung up."

"And it takes two of you?" This time looking at me.

"Apparently," I say.

Grahame refocuses on Ceo. "Well, chief. Here's my take on that. I don't think it's possible to calibrate a GPS. And even if it is, you don't have the skills to calibrate a freaking sock puppet."

A slow smile spreads across Ceo's face. He takes the GPS out of his pocket, stands up, and walks over to Grahame. Hands it to him and asks, "What does it say, *mon*?"

"It's searching."

"What's the elevation?"

"Sixty-two five."

"Do you know what elevation we're at?"

"Over seven?"

"More like over eight. Let me see it."

Grahame returns the GPS.

Ceo holds it out and rotates slowly while studying the display. He does a complete 360, plus a little more. Then he stops, gives Ellie a look, winds up, and hurls it into the fog.

I don't hear it land.

After a stunned beat, Grahame says, "What the hell, chief?"

Ceo says without the trace of a smile, "*That's* how I calibrate sock puppets. Any questions?"

Grahame raises his hand. "Please tell me you brought a compass."

Ceo laughs. "Why would I do that if I have a *freaking GPS*?"

He waits a few seconds, then starts walking down from the summit.

Grahame shouts at his back, "Hey, asswipe! What's the freaking plan *now*?"

"I'm going to find us a way out of this cloud."

G rahame coughs and says, "Someone's boyfriend has serious anger issues. He needs a better therapist."

Ellie says, "Not my boyfriend."

"Then what is he?"

She senses a shift in his tone. Something darker. "We've done this already."

"Well, whatever therapy he got last night didn't work."

"Shut up."

"I'm just saying you're a really good goalie, and he's used to scoring. A man in his deprived state should not be making life-or-death decisions."

Ellie fights the urge to walk five feet and punch him. It's a battle she's seconds from losing.

Colin says, "Grahame. You need to stop talking."

"You think I'm wrong?"

"Seriously. Stop talking."

"Not until I know what your problem is."

"All right. I think that what you said is offensive."

"Really? Considering that we're on top of a mountain in a freezing death cloud with no GPS, do you really think Ceo should be calling the shots?"

"I think you should apologize to Ellie."

"Ah, so *dat's* dee important ting to you, eh, mon?"

"Why are you doing this?"

"Doing what?"

"Being a dick. I mean, more than normal."

He smiles. "I've got reasons. But you made a good point." Back to Ellie, he says, "I apologize if what I said offended you."

And there it is again. The change in tone. It reminds her of Grahame on the bus, when his hand covered hers and he wouldn't let go. She says, "It did offend me, which makes the qualifier *if* invalid. I reject your insincere apology."

"See that, Q?" Grahame says. "That's why she's so awesome. Unlike you, she just doesn't take any shit." He stands, walks over to her, and says looking down, "What I said was inappropriate. I apologize for being a dick."

Ellie says, "The dick part I believe. Not the rest of it."

"Well, that's a start. But I stand by my original deal. Ceo is making some bad calls. The problem is you guys keep lining up at the trough." He starts pacing back and forth despite the ice, stirring wisps of gray in his wake. This movement could be to keep warm, she thinks, *or nerves.*

Colin says, "We've made our decisions as a group."

"Oh, really? Whose idea was it to tell Coach that we'd be playing in a tournament in San Diego? And did we decide as a group to not fill out a wilderness permit? Now look at us. Do you think anyone else knows we're even up here?"

Colin hesitates. "Rhody knows."

Grahame laughs. "Rhody? He thinks we're at Cannabis Cove, which by the way doesn't even exist!" He says to Ellie, "You've been texting a lot. Did you tell anyone we're up here?"

She shakes her head, says after a steadying beat, "I told everyone I would be at Pepperdine this weekend. I even had a friend post pictures of me at the school on Instagram and Facebook. She's the only person that knows I'm in Yosemite, but she doesn't know where."

Colin looks at her, stunned. "You lied to your parents?"

She nods.

He says, "Well. We talked to that navy guy on the way up. At least someone knows we're here. We'll be okay."

"But you told them we'd be doing the Yosemite Falls trail," she says. "Or maybe North Dome. Or going to those lakes. You pretty much told them we'd be going everywhere but here."

Grahame says, shaking his head, "And now it's snowing. Mon, dis sheet gettin' deeper, don't cha know." He returns to his pack and sits down. Ellie hopes this means the attack is over. Or it could be he's reloading. She looks around them, at the cloud that sits on their world and refuses to leave. Feels the cold sinking in, layer by layer, and wonders about Colin. How he's holding up in that thin nylon jacket and the gardening gloves, which he has been studying ever since she said that she lied about Pepperdine. On a whim she pulls out her phone. No signal.

After a couple minutes, Grahame says, "Actually, there's a bright spot in this scenario. We may not be alone up here."

"What?" Colin says.

"While I was on my little walk I heard a couple of guys talking. I thought about introducing myself, but the topic of their conversation seemed a little...weird."

After a beat, Colin says, "What were they talking about?"

"Kitchen appliances, of all things."

"And what kind of appliances would those be?"

"I distinctly heard the words *blender* and *kitten* a couple of times. I know. Weird, huh? That got me a little worried. So I decided to look for you guys. Luckily I found Ellie." He looks at her, eyebrows knitted in concern. "Sorry about scaring you, but there's some weird shit going on. I should've known you'd be all jumpy."

Ellie had never seen Colin's expression so hard, so still. Like his features were sculpted from one of these boulders. She considers the odds of two other men being up here, on this day, in this weather, and determines that they're beyond imagining. Which makes her wonder what a blender and calibrating a GPS have in common. Colin has barely looked at her since he returned, and that's what is eating at her center more than anything else.

She asks, "Colin? What am I missing here?"

He works those gloves.

Grahame kicks at a stone.

The snowflakes continue to fall around them. A few more now than a minute ago. One lands on Ellie's jacket. Another on her pack. Just when she thinks it's going to really start falling—they stop.

Ellie thinks about Ceo's words *if the weather turns.*

And his voice calls out from below, "Strap on your packs, race fans. Time to go home."

THE STORM

48

COLIN

Lunch is a three-minute cram session of dried apricots, beef jerky, and a few swigs of water from our dwindling supply. We follow Ceo down a section of the summit ridge where he says the rock has more texture so the icing isn't as bad. I manage with my sneakers, but it isn't easy. The big toes on both feet are bordering on blocks of ice.

We turn left and head down the Snow Creek Trail side of the ridge. That much I know for sure because the other side of the ridge leads down to Tenaya Canyon, a place we absolutely don't want to go. It's an unnerving sensation, walking down a slope where I could slip and potentially fall an unknown distance. It could be ten feet or one hundred. There could be a cliff, or a tree, or even a bear at the bottom. I have no idea. I think we made the left further up the ridge than when we crested this morning—but like everything else, it's just a feeling with no point of reference to orient my head. The cloud is just as thick down here as it was at the top. Ellie says it's worse. She's probably right.

The terrain goes from steep to moderately sloping granite to an easy mixture of granite and trees. As the angle decreases, my traction improves and I don't have to focus so much on where I put every single step. We stay in a tight line, Ceo, me, Ellie, and Grahame. Our progress is slow, since, thanks again to my footwear issues, we continually have to work our way around the rocky patches. The end result is a creeping sensation that we're meandering rather than heading in a purposeful direction. Amazingly, Grahame has said *Me tinks dah GPS would be ah nice ting to have, eh, mon* only once.

Ceo's plan (which we all agreed on) is to keep walking until we hit Snow Creek, then follow it downstream to the bridge. From that point, finding our way to the switchbacks will be easy. He says if we miss the creek, there is a trail that circles around the north side of Watkins, and we should be watching for that, too. The problem is how long this march is taking. We left the summit a little after one. It must be well after two by now, maybe closer to three. By my calculation, we should have intersected the Snow Creek Trail by now.

Meanwhile, along with everything else, I'm thinking about what Grahame said at the summit. He obviously overheard me and Ceo talking, although I don't know if he heard everything Ceo said. I have to assume he heard enough to figure things out. That would explain why Grahame went off on Ceo and all his decisions. He doesn't like being played by him—*ever*, and Ceo played us all from the start. I haven't had a chance to tell Ceo that Grahame knows about his scheme. I'm hoping to get that chance before Grahame unloads on him. Which he will definitely do. That clock is already ticking. I also think that Ellie suspects something is amiss after

Grahame told that bizarre story about overhearing two random guys talking about blenders. She basically asked me flat out, *What am I missing here?* I hated not telling her the truth and how that truth changes everything. It's Ceo's job to go there, not mine.

The more we walk, the more some of the terrain is starting to look disturbingly familiar. We just passed a tree with a lump on it that I swear I've seen before. Maybe we passed it on the way up, but what are those odds? This adds to my growing apprehension that we have absolutely no clue where we are. Looking at the ridiculously simple trail map, without contour lines or the benefit of visual landmarks, is a waste of time. Grahame has a better word for our state. He calls out from the back of the line, "Hey, chief! Are we freaking lost?"

Ceo stops.

We gather in a sagging clump, breathing heavy and sweating despite the cold, while Ceo takes off a glove and pulls out the trail map. He studies it for the fifth time since leaving the summit, rubs his chin.

"It's like a bad hand in poker," Grahame says. "No matter how long you stare at it, it just *ain't gonna change.*"

"You are the wrong person to be handing out poker tips." Ceo points to a spot on the map. "I know we're somewhere in here, between the creek and Mount Watkins. I thought we were headed west. I honestly don't know anymore."

"It feels to me like we're circling," Ellie says.

"Me too," I say.

"That's possible, but I'm pretty sure we're not."

"Pretty sure?" Grahame says. "Well, guess what? I'm pretty sure we're *fucked.*"

They exchange dark looks.

I say, "How much daylight do we have left?"

Ceo looks at his watch. "It's three seventeen. We have an hour before it starts getting dark."

He said during lunch that we'd be switchbacking our way down by three.

We all let that sink in.

"Any luck with a cell signal?" he asks.

Grahame and Ellie check their phones, shake their heads. I don't even bother.

"I guess that leaves us with two options. Look for a place to camp and find the trail tomorrow. Or keep walking and hope we get lucky and hit the trail before dark."

"And what direction, O wise one, would that be?" Grahame asks.

"Whatever direction you pick."

"Is there a third option?" Grahame says.

Ellie says, "We could try yelling for help."

"Great idea," Grahame says. "All that will do is attract the bears."

"We're wasting time," Ceo says. "Before we make any decisions, how are we set for water?"

We do a count, and between the four of us, we have two full quarts and a half of Ceo's CamelBak. He says that should last us until we hit the creek. During that process a soft drizzle starts to fall. I'm surprised this isn't snow. If we're not at the freezing mark, we can't be far from it. This new development reduces our two options by 50 percent. We find a clearing nearby at the bottom of a small slope and set up the tents. Ceo takes the ax and brings back a couple of dripping limbs. They're too wet to start a fire. We don't hang the food because we cut up the rope to stake out our pathetic rain fly, so we leave it in a stuff sack on top of a boulder. By the time we crawl into our respective tents and I have to face Ceo spending yet another night with Ellie, on top of everything else, the drizzle switches gears. Now it's a steady pounding rain.

Grahame and I pull off our soaked clothes down to the skin and crawl shivering into our cold sleeping bags. From there we watch water collect on the pathetic rain fly, which is sagging already. The water creates mini rivers that form mini waterfalls that pour through the exposed mosquito mesh and onto the floor of our tent. I already feel it soaking through the end of my bag.

Grahame says through chattering teeth, "Want to know my three wishes for today?"

"That we didn't leave the toilet paper outside?" I say, having no idea where this list is headed, but certain that I won't like it when I get there.

"Nah. I'll just use one of your socks. Number three is I wish I was in our dorm room studying for the ASVAB instead of freezing to death in the world's crappiest tent."

"Okay. What's number two?"

"I wish we hadn't let Ceo talk us into climbing that mountain."

"Roger that."

"Ready for wish number one?"

"Make it quick. My organs are shutting down."

"I wish it wasn't so foggy today. You know why?"

"Why?"

"That way I could've snapped a picture of your face when Ceo said the whole reason he talked us into this fucking trip was to hook you up with goalie girl." He laughs between shivers. "Dog, I'd turn that into a poster and never it take down."

49
ELLIE

With the rain bouncing off their tent. With the gray day outside sliding into night and his sleeping bag pressed against hers. With their conversation not on the storm but on everything else because talking about the shit they're in now won't *change a thing.* With all that behind them and winding down to the improbability of sleep he asks, "You warm yet?"

"Almost."

"Do you need any of my clothes?"

"I'm good."

"Don't be trying to score my comfy socks."

"Your socks are safe."

He goes quiet for a while. Then rolls onto his side, facing her.

It's so black in here she can't see him, but she feels the touch of his breath on her face.

He says, "You've been quiet way over there in Ellie land. What's on your mind?"

She considers all the thoughts in her head. Colin in that leaking tent and all the rain. How he looked so wet and cold, like a cat pulled out of a well. About what his night will be compared to hers. About the withering look he gave Ceo. About the prospects of tomorrow and the odds that the weather will clear enough so they can find their way out of this forest. About her parents and the conversation waiting for her when this part is over. She puts it all into a mental list, ranks them in order of priority and the number one spot is occupied by two words:

"Kitchen appliances."

"Wow." A laugh rolls out of the dark. "Did not see that coming."

"What's your favorite?"

"My favorite kitchen appliance? Hmmm . . . that's a tough one. There are so many good choices. Most guys would go with the microwave. For me it's a tie between espresso machines and dishwashers."

"If you had to pick one?"

"Espresso machines. Doing dishes is optional. Caffeine is not."

"Funny," she says, "I had you pegged for something totally different."

"Not a garbage disposal, I hope."

"I heard you're a blender guy."

She counts ten seconds before he says, "Who told you that?"

"Grahame."

"When?"

"After you threw the GPS off a cliff."

"What else did he say?"

"He said you need a new therapist."

"A new therapist?"

"As in the therapy you got from me last night didn't work."

Ceo rolls onto his back. After a deep sigh he tells her, "I'm sorry Grahame said that. And he will be, too. That's a promise."

He turns away, his back to her.

The silence in their tent drowns out the infinite drum of rain.

50
COLIN

Grahame nudges me with an elbow.

Whispers, "You hear that?"

"Hear what?"

"Shh. On the boulder."

I listen.

The first thing I notice is that the rain has stopped. It's a different sound. Not the splat of rain. Soft, like petals falling on skin. Something passes through the mesh and lands on my face. Cold and wet.

Snow.

Then I hear the other sounds.

A snort. A grunt.

Claws scraping on rock.

My heart surges against my ribs.

Grahame hisses, *"Oh shit oh shit."*

Cloth tearing.

Boxes shredded, cans rolling down.

We listen to it feed.

Then nothing.

Padded feet in mud.

Is it still hungry?

Fur brushing our tent.

The side next to me bulges in against my head.

It pauses.

The fabric relaxes.

Silence.

Minutes pass.

Snow falls.

Grahame finally whispers, "Is it gone?"

"I think so."

"Dude, it was inches from your head."

"Yeah."

"My feet felt like a couple of rib eyes."

"At least they were frozen," I say.

"Dumb-ass me leaves the ax outside."

"And Smokey lives another day."

After a bit he says, "The end of my bag is soaked."

"Mine too. I think we put our tent in the runoff from that hill."

"How is it without a sleeping pad?"

"It's like sleeping on an Eskimo pie. There's a dry spot under my left elbow."

He laughs at our comedy of errors. "This trip can't get worse. Right?"

Something breaks loose and slides down the rain fly.

I reach up, tap on the roof. It unleashes an avalanche.

I sit up in the cold. Grope for my headlamp, switch it on.

My breath clouds in the beam. I open the door. Aim it out into the dark.

Big flakes falling through the trees. Lots of them.

The ground is white. Totally white. Except for the footprints. The footprints passing next to our tent. They're still black. But already filling in.

"Sorry to break the news," I say, reaching for the water bottle.

It's frozen solid.

"This trip is officially worse."

51
ELLIE

Later, after the rain changed to snow. After the bear. After the wind. After the dream where Colin is in her room in a pink towel looking for the soap under her bed, Ceo asks Ellie what she thinks of Q.

Her eyes fly open.

"Before you answer that," he says, "I have something to tell you."

52

COLIN

Morning can't come soon enough. But when it does it brings a sledgehammer.

The snow is piling up. The bear prints are long gone. The trees around us are vague shapes behind a curtain of white. And just as the gray light of dawn brings focus to the day, the wind is unleashed. It shakes and shudders the tent, claws at the rain fly, pops the stakeout lines, whips snow through the mosquito netting like flour through a sifter. I look at the other tent. Their fly is better, but not by much. One side already has a drift covering half the door. The branch that Ceo chopped is reduced to a white bump. I figure we've had six to eight inches, and our clearing is sheltered by trees. Make that ten inches out in the wide-open spaces where I would hate to face that wind. My stomach sinks as I realize that the trail will be covered. If it keeps falling at this rate, by the time we're all packed and ready to go, there will be close to a foot on the ground and much higher than that in the drifts. With the wind blowing like it is, who knows what the visibility will be. Worse than yesterday, that's for sure. And I'll be wading through it all in tennis shoes with holes in the toes.

I upgrade the task of trail finding from difficult to impossible.

Grahame hasn't spoken for the past hour. I know he's awake because his teeth are chattering.

I hear the sound of a zipper outside.

Ceo's hat-covered head emerges from the door. He punches through the drift and walks the ten feet to our tent, saying, "Good morning, lads. It's a fine, fine day in the neighborhood!"

All he gets from our tent is a collective groan.

Ceo crouches down, raises the rain fly, and peers in. His eyes darken as he surveys our world. He says, "It's like the *Titanic* in here."

I say, "We're in the runoff from that hill."

"That's some bad luck," he says.

"No...shhhhh...shit," Grahame says between convulsive shivers.

"You guys hang in. I'll be right back."

He drops the rain fly and leaves.

Ceo returns a few minutes later, unzips the door to our tent in a blast of wind and snow. He tosses Grahame his sleeping bag, then hands me two stuff sacks and his sleeping pad. "Grahame, your bag is soaked. Use mine. It's Gore-Tex, so it won't get wet. Q, the small sack is a waterproof bivy. Put your sleeping bag inside it. You won't get dry, but at least you'll preserve body heat. My foam pad should help. The first thing is you all need to get dry and warm. I have extra socks and a sweater in the big stuff sack. I'll be back."

"Where are you going?" Grahame says, pulling off his shirt.

"To start a fire."

"In a freaking blizzard?"

"Not a problem," Ceo says. "With a little help from Team Coleman."

The fire roars and snaps. It rages against the howling wind and stinging snow that are determined to snuff it out. Ceo had to use most of the remaining Coleman fuel from his stove to get it started. He's saving the rest of the fuel in case this fire goes out. No point in saving it for food because the stove wouldn't start and the bear ate it all except for one small tin of chicken meat with a puncture hole in the top. We shared it out of the can. The four of us huddle around the flames in a tight U, shoulder to shoulder, backs to the wind, holding out our wet clothes, hoping they will dry. This isn't the best arrangement because the wind carries away most of the heat. If we move, the fire will be overcome by the storm and die.

Ceo's sweater under my jacket makes a huge difference. I know he's giving up an important part of his layering system, but he insisted. He's worried about my feet, and so am I. My rain-soaked sneakers were frozen stiff when I put them on. Steam rises off them now with my toes four inches from the flames. I keep remembering that old guy in the navy cap we met on the way up, the way he stared at my sneakers a little too long. Now I know why.

My gloves were frozen, too, but they have thawed and are starting to dry. Ellie is standing beside me, gloved hands out like mine over the flames. She's keeping her words to a minimum, just like the rest of us. I have no idea what went on in their tent last night. Maybe Ceo told her about what he's done. If he did, I can't tell by looking at her. Anyway, I don't have the energy to think about it. The reality of our situation is too dire to deal with anything else.

Ceo drops another snowy log on the fire. He says over the hissing flames, "Anyone want to try hiking out?"

I say, "We can't risk getting lost in this."

"I agree," Ellie says.

"So we're waiting out the storm here," Ceo says. "Are we all on that page?"

Grim nods.

Ceo says, "The wind has shredded one of the tents and—"

"And a bear ate all our food; we're almost out of water. So in other words, we're fucked," Grahame says. "What's your point?"

"We need to build a shelter."

"*Build a shelter?* What's wrong with your tent?"

"It's a one-person ultra-light."

"We'll cram inside."

"It's not designed for this weather. Or that many bodies. It won't hold up."

"So what?" Grahame says. "You want to build a freaking igloo?"

"Yes."

"This is the wrong kind of snow for an igloo," I say. "I used to build them with my father when we went ice fishing. This snow isn't deep enough or hard enough to cut blocks."

"What about a snow cave?" Ellie says.

"Same problem," Ceo says. "Not enough snow."

"So, like I said," Grahame says. "We're fu—"

"We heard you the first time," Ceo says. "We'll get through this. But we all—"

"We all wouldn't have to get *through this*," Grahame says, spitting his words, "if it weren't for you insisting that we had to climb that mountain."

"I didn't insist."

"You saw all the clouds. You knew the weather was turning to shit. But then you lied to us just like you always do, and here we are. Freezing to death in a blizzard in the middle of freaking *nowhere*!"

"I didn't lie to you."

"Every word, mon. Every fucking word."

I know where that's coming from, and it chills me deeper than the wind. I keep hoping for a chance to warn Ceo. It needs to happen soon, but I don't see how.

Ceo kicks at the fire. The logs shift and fall, sending a column of sparks up and away. Across the fire is the boulder where we had our food. I've been looking at the two trees framing it on either side. They're about six feet apart.

I say, "Did anyone see the movie *The Edge*?"

53

ELLIE

"Anthony Hopkins and Alex Baldwin, 1997," she says, picturing the scene he's probably thinking about. Three men huddled under a small structure made of branches, twigs, and rope. Rain in sheets coming down, water leaking in, soaked to the bone.

Grahame says, "I did. A dude gets eaten by a bear."

"Mauled," Colin says. "Not eaten."

"He died from it, right?"

"Eventually. But that's not the point."

"The point is," Grahame says, "your idea sucked before you said it."

Ellie tenses at the force behind Grahame's words. She thinks: Am I the only one seeing this?

"What about the movie?" Ceo asks.

"Three guys survive a plane crash in a remote lake in Alaska. They build a lean-to and the only tools they have are a knife and some rope."

"And a paper clip and a silk handkerchief," she says, wondering if Colin will smile at this. He does, for a moment. And despite everything, her mind is gripped with the impact of what Ceo said about Colin last night.

"How do we build it?" Ceo asks.

Colin points across the flames. "We could use those two trees over there. Wedge a log horizontally between them and the boulder."

"What do we use for the roof and sides?"

"Lots of branches. Maybe dig for pine needles under the snow."

"Are you *insane*?" Grahame says. "That'll take forever. We'll freeze to death digging around in this snow looking for pine needles."

Ellie sees Colin struggle for an answer. As if he has to choose between thinking and fighting off the wind. She says, "How about the tents and rain flies? We can use the poles for support, then we put snow on top of it."

Ceo looks at Colin.

Colin nods and shivers. "I like it." He sends a fleeting smile her way.

"I vote we go with Q's plan." Ceo turns to face Grahame. "Are you on that page?"

"I'm on any page," Grahame says, his eyes blazing back at Ceo, "as long as you didn't write it."

54

COLIN

Ceo, after a good hard look at Grahame, says to me and Ellie, "You guys transfer all the gear from the wet tent into the dry one. Then break it down and put it someplace that won't blow away. After that, start hauling in branches. But don't go too far and don't get lost."

"What about the fire?" I ask, thinking about my sneakers plowing through that snow, and worried about the only hope I have to relieve the pain in my feet.

"Let it go. We'll build another one as soon as the shelter is done."

"What are you and I doing?" Grahame asks.

Ceo shoulders the ax.

"Your favorite thing. We're gonna chop some shit."

Grahame follows him into the white.

The wind already filling in the footsteps behind them.

55
COLIN

I crawl into the tent, hand our soggy gear out to Ellie. She makes the twenty-foot trudge to Ceo's tent, dumps the gear inside, and returns for another load. It takes four trips, during which the fire turns into a snow-covered heap. We dig out the stakes for the rain fly while the storm, as if sensing that we intend to fight it, intensifies around us. Visibility shrinks from a hundred feet to fifty feet. Just as we're breaking down the poles and tent and wrapping it all inside the rain fly, Ceo and Grahame return with three logs. They are hunched over and covered with snow. Grahame's thick black eyebrows are crusted with ice.

Ceo asks, "Are these big enough?"

They're about eight to ten feet long, one with fresh branches that Ceo knocks off with the ax. The other two look like they've been dead for years. None of them are straight, but they'll work.

"Yes," I say.

"How many more?"

"Two."

Grahame looks at the dead fire and groans.

Ceo says to Ellie, "How're you holding up?"

"Better than Colin."

"Ha. This is a shorts and T-shirt day in Vermont." Then he says to Grahame, "Your pick this time."

"Let me go with you," I say, thinking this may be the best chance I get to warn him about Grahame.

Ceo says, "Not with those shoes. You stay here and build us a home."

Grahame walks up to me, says in my ear, *"Kittens in a blender."*

He walks away.

Ceo follows him into the woods.

56

ELLIE

She works with Colin to build the frame for their shelter. They use the shortest log for the horizontal support that rests on the boulder and spans between the two trees. They lift the other two logs and lean them diagonally at opposite ends, creating a wedge-shaped frame. One of the logs is bent and keeps slipping off. They use a piece of rope to tie it down. Colin has to remove his gloves to fasten the knot. His fingers are too stiff. He asks Ellie to do it for him. She notices that his movements are becoming increasingly slow and methodical. His speech is down to a minimum, and when he does talk, the sentences are short.

He says, "Branches now."

She says, "You need to be out of this wind. Get into one of the sleeping bags. I'll get the branches."

"Can't separate. Too dangerous. You go first."

"Which way?"

"Wind to our backs. In case we can't find our prints. We'll know which way to go."

They walk for maybe five minutes, stopping to tear off any branches within reach. Dead or alive, it doesn't matter. With their arms nearly full and their tracks beginning to fill in, she looks at him and wonders how he's still standing. She says, "Let's head back."

"Okay."

They walk for a while. The flat light is turning gray. It's happening too fast. She asks him if he brought his headlamp. He says, No, you? She tells him no.

He attempts a smile, tells her they'll make it.

57

COLIN

We're almost there. The first thing I see is the tent, a bubble of orange and yellow. Then a dark shape hunched over, pacing back and forth. This shape is too big to be Ceo. A haunting sound reaches them, like a lone wolf howling into the wind.

I say, "Something's wrong."

Grahame stops and turns.

Ellie says, "What happened to his jacket?"

I try to run. The snow is too deep. I fall facedown. Try to stand, fall again. Ellie helps me up. Then we're both running. We make it to camp, stop and stare at Grahame, our eyes wide in shock and horror.

His coat is stained dark. His pants, his gloves, his *face*.

I know it's blood. Everywhere.

Ellie screams.

I yell at Grahame, "What happened?"

"It . . . it was an accident. I didn't mean . . ."

"Didn't mean what? What accident? What are you talking about?"

He stands there, a block of ice in the wind.

"Say something!" I grab his shoulders and shake him. Clumps of red fall off his jacket to the ground. "What the hell did you do?"

"I hit him."

"Hit him with what?"

He looks to his left.

My arms fall. I back away. The ax is leaning against a rock. I stare at the handle, see the blood. "Oh shit. Where did you hit him?"

He stares at me, black eyes rimmed with red.

"Where did you hit him?"

"In the face, Q. I hit Ceo in the fucking face. He's dead."

Ellie moans, Oh God oh God oh God, as my head spins.

Grahame drops to his knees and sobs.

58

COLIN

He won't get up no matter what I do or say.

I have to find something that works. Kick him, drag him, whatever it takes. The wind is erasing his tracks. Without his help, I'll never find Ceo. Not in time anyway.

Ellie says, "What are you going to do?"

"I'm going to find Ceo."

"How?"

"Grahame."

"But he's worthless!"

I look at him, still on his knees, still facedown in the snow. He mutters *accident* over and over between shuddering moans. "Then I'll find him myself."

"You can't do that."

"I have to. While there's still tracks left."

"Colin. Listen to me. You *can't* go."

"I'll be back."

"What about the shelter?"

"Use the tent."

"What if you get lost?"

"I won't."

"Look around you, Colin! It's a whiteout. You can hardly walk. You're probably hypothermic. We need to get out of this wind."

"Ellie! This isn't a choice!"

"Then you'll die looking for someone that's already dead."

Her words sting worse than the driving snow. It takes a moment to recover.

"You don't know that," I say.

"He hit him in the head, Colin. You know how strong he is. You saw all the blood."

"Not the head. He said the *face*. Face wounds bleed a lot." I shove Grahame hard with the heel of my foot. *"Get up!"*

He moans but doesn't stand.

I crouch down next to him and yell, "Get up, asshole! We need to find Ceo." Nothing changes. I stand, face Ellie. "You're right. He's worthless. I'm going."

I start to turn.

She grabs my arm, spins me around. Her eyes find mine. They're jittery, swimming with fear. I'm scared, too. But my fear comes from confusion, shock. My best friend is lost and bleeding in the storm. By the way she looks at me, by the rigid set to her jaw, I know her fear comes from a different place.

Ellie yanks me back and back, away from Grahame.

"What about *me*?" she says.

"What do you mean?"

"What if you go off with him? And..."

"And what?"

"And he comes back. But *you don't*."

My mind is too numb to follow her down this path. Or maybe it just doesn't want to.

Her eyes drill into mine. She moves closer and lowers her voice. "Think about it. How do you hit someone in the face with an ax? By *mistake*?"

"I don't know. He said that's what happened."

"And you believe it?"

"Yes." Then finally her fear breaks through and starts chipping away at mine.

"Are you saying—"

She raises a finger to her lips.

I stop, listen. All I hear is the wind. Grahame isn't moaning. I turn around.

He's risen up out of the snow, facing us. The stain on his jacket and pants has turned to black. He says in a voice as flat and empty as a frozen lake, "I'm tired. I'll show you the body in the morning."

Grahame starts to walk toward the tent, then stops and returns for the ax.

"Hey!" I yell. "We need that!"

Either he didn't hear me or chooses to ignore what I said. Grahame kicks through drifts all the way to Ceo's tent. He unzips the fly, crawls inside. The flap zips shut.

Ellie releases my arm.

Snow stings my face.

I can't feel my feet.

The storm howls in victory.

59

ELLIE

Ellie works with Colin to finish the lean-to because Ceo's tent is *occupied* and she refuses its shelter even if it means freezing to death. The wind is an impatient beast raging around them, whipping the rain fly from Colin's tent so hard that it cuts his hand. Branches blow away before their numb fingers can tie them down with pieces of nearly frozen rope. A task that should take minutes takes an hour at least. She thinks about curling up in the snow, believing if she lets it pile up and around like a blanket, somehow warmth will find her, or at least the relentless pain in her hands and feet will recede into a dull ache. That has to be better than this. She tells her plan to Colin. He says he hasn't felt his feet since they started building this shelter and that is *not* a good thing.

He refuses to stop. He says the storm will not win. It's hard to tell how much light is left, so let's not waste it. At one point, when it looks like there will be no roof and therefore no shelter, he disappears into Ceo's tent and returns with the bungee cords from Grahame's pack. Combined with rope, compression straps from the packs, and tent poles woven between the branches, they build a roof that holds long enough to weight it with snow. They use a foam sleeping pad and the toilet shovel to pile snow against the sides until it is high enough to cover all the holes except for an opening on the leeward side. They crawl into the shelter, collapse in the snow. The sound of their heaving chests is all that penetrates the blessed calm.

She eventually says, "I'm so tired. Can we stay like this?" Realizes she is shouting, quietly rephrases, "We don't have to go outside again, right?"

Colin answers, "We're going to hunker down and wait out the storm. But I have something to do first. I'll be back. Don't fall asleep."

"Get the ax. Please."

"I will."

She's too tired to ask him what it is he has to do, or where he's going, or why she can't sleep. Sleeping is all she wants to do. "Come back," is all she can say.

Ellie reaches out to touch him.

All she feels is snow.

60

COLIN

Grahame watches in silence from the comfort of Ceo's down-filled sleeping bag while I stuff my pack with the gear Ellie and I need to survive this night. It won't be easy. The bottom third of my bag is still soaked from the rain this morning, and Grahame's is worse. I have to get back to Ellie, but this process is taking longer than it should. My fingers are too numb to perform simple tasks like closing zippers and tying knots. Plus I'm trying to avoid the stained jacket on the floor next to Grahame, and not look at the gloves in the mesh pocket above his head, frozen stiff with Ceo's blood.

When I'm finally done, Grahame says, "There were branches sticking up."

"What?"

"On a log. Sticking up out of the snow."

This can't be happening. "Not now, Grahame."

"She can wait a little. You have to hear this."

"Okay," I say, desperate to leave, but knowing that he's right. "You get one minute."

He closes his eyes, talks in a near-dead monotone. "We were cold and tired. Nothing looked familiar. Just snow and trees. Ceo kept saying, 'It has to be around here somewhere, it has to be around here somewhere.' I thought he was talking about the creek. Then we passed two trees that form a big V. The log was about forty feet from there."

"The one with the branches?"

Grahame opens his eyes, nods.

"Was he looking for that log?"

"I don't think so. That would be just too weird. Anyway, Ceo wants the branches gone so it will be easier to drag back to camp. He gives me the ax and says, 'You like to chop stuff—be my guest.'" Grahame pauses, takes a breath. "So I walk up to the log, tell him to stand behind me, then I . . . then I . . . instead of chopping down, I try to take out all those branches with one big golf swing. My feet slip in the snow. I totally miss the branches, and my follow-through comes around . . . and . . . and the ax hits him square in the face." Grahame's eyes find mine again. This time they're rimmed with tears. I want to tell him your minute's up. But he's ready to speak, and there's no escaping now. I have to hear the rest.

Grahame says, "It was like slicing into an avocado. I felt the bone breaking up through the handle. He fell back, moaning, his gloves covering his face. At first there was nothing and I thought he was okay. Then there was blood. So much blood. It happened so fast. I was screaming what have I done, what have I done?" He takes another breath. "When he fell he was sitting up. By the time I could move he was on his back. I . . . sat next to him, put his head on my lap. I didn't know what else to do. His hands were in the way. I kept asking him to move them so I could look. See if his nose was still there. But he wouldn't do it. The blood...the snow...that fucking wind. Then he made a gurgling sound. Like he was choking. I turned his head to the side thinking it was the blood in his mouth. That he couldn't breathe. As soon as I did that his body started shaking. After a few seconds he went stiff, and then...and then the choking stopped. He goes limp. He wasn't moving or making any sounds." Grahame shakes his head.

I'm trembling. Barely able to talk.

"Did you feel for a pulse?"

"Yes," he says. "But there was so much snow, my hands were cold..."

"What did you feel?"

"Nothing. I felt nothing."

"But you don't know for sure."

"He died, Q. Right there in my arms. All that blood. There's just no way—"

"Your minute's up. I need to go."

"Wait." He squirms around inside Ceo's sleeping bag. Comes out with a pair of something that looks like puffy down slippers. "They're Ceo's. My feet are finally warm." I hesitate, wanting them, but not feeling right about it. Grahame tosses them to me. "You know he'd want you to wear them, even if he was alive."

He is alive. I stuff them inside my coat.

"There's one more thing." Grahame's arm slips out of his sleeping bag. He reaches for his jacket, searches through the pockets, then hands me two jalapeño Slim Jims. "For you and the one that doesn't believe me."

"Thanks," I say, knowing what this means. Slim Jims are Ceo's favorite food. Since they were in Grahame's jacket, that means he must have gone through Ceo's clothes at the scene.

"It was an accident, Q. I know that bi—I know she doesn't believe me. But you do. Right?"

After a beat, "Yeah, sure."

Thinking, No I don't.

I yank my pack toward the door. The movement shifts Ceo's jacket, exposing the ax. I almost forgot about it. I reach for the handle. Grahame tries to block me with his arm. I knock it away.

"Don't," he says.

I strap the ax to my pack.

"Let me keep it here. *Please!*"

His eyes are wide with fear. What is he thinking? That I'm going to sneak in here and do to him what he did to Ceo? Whatever his problem is, I don't care.

I say, "Stay away from us."

And can't get out of that tent fast enough.

61

ELLIE

He shakes Ellie till she knows it's him.

She watches from some far-off place while he puts foam pads over the snow, pulls sleeping bags from his pack, spreads them on top of the pads, undoes zippers, wipes away chunks of white that fall when his head brushes the roof. He unlaces and removes her boots, tugs off her wet socks. Wet pants slide down and off. Something soft goes over her feet. He tells her to get into the bag. She crawls in, shivering so hard she thinks her bones will snap.

Hears him moving next to her, teeth chattering in the almost-dark.

Swearing at the cold as if it has a beating heart.

His arm sliding into her sleeping bag, around her chest, pulling her to him.

Shivering together.

Slowly, like a sliver of sunlight leaking under a curtain spreading gold against her bedroom wall.

Warmth finds them.

Her body returns to the rhythms she knows.

The fury of the world outside is lost, and it is just the two of them in this shelter of wood and snow and pieces of broken tent.

As conscious thought seeps in, she asks, "Did you get the ax?"

"Yes. Shh..."

Minutes or hours later, she asks him from what must be a dream, "What did you put on my feet?"

"Magic slippers."

"Mmmmmmm."

She rides them to a beach in Fiji.

62

COLIN

I punch through a drift that nearly fills the opening to our shelter. I did the same thing twice last night, afraid the opening would be covered completely and we would run out of air.

It's a world transformed. The gray and green and brown landscape that started this journey has turned into a smooth, pristine white. The weather has changed, too. Snow isn't falling, and there is no fog, so I can see deep into the trees. It feels warmer outside, maybe close to the freezing mark already. Best of all, the wind is reduced to swirling ghosts of powder. They skim across the surface, as if sent to smooth out the final traces of our prints from yesterday. Looking at the scooped-out bases around the trees, and the thick coating of snow on Ceo's tent, I figure Mother Nature dumped another four inches on us overnight. That puts her total somewhere between twelve and twenty. I look up, see the clouds, and know in a sickening instant that she isn't finished with this canvas.

"So?" Ellie asks, waiting for my report.

"We need to get out of here."

* * *

I'm anxious to start our search for Ceo. Before that can happen we need more water. Not a lot, so it won't take long. Just enough to reach Snow Creek plus some extra for Ceo when we find him. Which we will. I've been mentally preparing for that event ever since I untangled myself from Ellie this morning and she whispered, *Thanks for being my heater.* Thinking about the grim prospects ahead, those five words from her will surely be the best thing I hear all day.

Ellie helps me build the fire with leftover wood from the lean-to and the last of the Coleman fuel. Initially it flares up like a bomb, then the fuel burns off in less than a minute and the roaring flames turn into smoking embers. Ellie crouches down to snow level and blows softly on the little dots of orange while I add twigs and pine needles one at a time until the flames catch and we have a steady fire. I fill a cooking pot with snow, bridge it over two rocks. We chew on the jalapeño Slim Jims while waiting for the snow to melt.

The fact that Grahame is not up and packed, like we are, grates on me. He knows I can't do this without him and that every second counts. I think about shaking his tent and yelling, *Enough of this shit.*

Then Ellie bends over and coughs.

I heard it a couple times last night, and a few more this morning. She says she's okay, it's just an itch, but the rattle in her chest says otherwise. Add this new development to Ceo's unknown state, a brooding sky, and my feet, which are numb already—and I can't take it anymore.

I say, "Screw it. I'm waking him up."

"Wait," Ellie says in a hushed tone, "you guys talked yesterday. Did Grahame tell you his side?"

"Yes. It was a hard thing to hear."

"What did he say?"

I tell her everything, including the part where Ceo kept looking for something but he wouldn't tell Grahame what it was. When I'm finished, she studies the fire for a full minute. Then her eyebrows gather in concern, and she says, "On our first night, when Grahame chopped a huge limb off that dead tree—he told me to stand behind him."

"That makes sense."

"He told Ceo the same thing."

"So it fits."

"Not quite. The difference is when he hit that log in front of me, he chopped down like a pro. He knew exactly what he was doing. This time is different. He swings in a circle. And misses everything—*except* Ceo's head."

"It was a blizzard, Ellie. He said he slipped."

"I know. That explains why he missed the branches and hit Ceo by accident. But that doesn't expla—" And she coughs several times. It sounds like marbles are loose in her lungs. After it passes, she dials her voice down to a throaty whisper: "It doesn't explain why he swung in a circle. He could have slipped, like he said. Or Ceo could have moved and . . ." She leaves her thought unfinished.

"Ellie, I know what you're saying. But Grahame isn't like that. There's no way he would do it. Not on purpose. I saw him last night. He was close to tears." I don't tell her about the Slim Jims.

Or what Grahame whispered to me before walking with Ceo into the woods.

Kittens in a blender.

I thought he was just reminding me about what Ceo did. As if I'd forget. But maybe it was something more than that. Maybe Ceo had pushed him one too many times.

Ellie says, "Think about all that's happened. The bet, the race, Cannabis Cove? Tossing the GPS over a cliff. He blames Ceo for everything. Plus there's some things I didn't tell you."

"Like what?"

"He made a pass at me. Twice."

"When?"

"On the shuttle bus. He trapped my hand under his and wouldn't let go. It was a creepy-cousin kind of thing. Then again that night, when I was up at the log trying to go to the bathroom. He asked me if I wanted to kick Ceo out of the tent and sleep with him."

"He had to be joking."

"He wasn't. There's something dark about him. Seriously dark."

I look at her, hoping that she's done. But I can tell by the grim set of her lips she isn't. "Is there more?"

"Do you remember when you, me, and Grahame were on the summit, and Grahame said that Ceo had anger-management issues because I wasn't giving him the right kind of therapy?"

"Yeah. That was bad, even for Grahame. You didn't..."

She nods.

"You *told* Ceo?"

"Yes."

"Why?"

"I don't know. I wish I didn't. But that doesn't matter now. What matters is what Ceo said."

"What did he say?"

"That he was sorry. Then he promised that Grahame would be sorry, too."

"Shit!" I kick at a clump of snow. It lands on a rock in the fire and hisses. Just like the resulting steam, I feel my anger rising. "So you're saying that Ceo—"

She grabs my arm, nods toward the tent, and whispers, "Shh!"

Lowering my voice, I say, "You're saying that Ceo confronted Grahame, and because of it, Grahame axed him in the face?"

Ellie says, "No, I'm not saying that. But it is a piece. And when you add all the pieces together, they don't equal an accident."

What she isn't factoring into her equation is the biggest piece of all. That Grahame overheard Ceo's grand plan to hook me up with Ellie. That makes me wonder if Ceo even told her about it. Now these new and disturbing developments—that Grahame had some twisted idea from the start that he could score with Ellie. And maybe Ceo had some payback in mind for something Grahame said. I'm considering the dangers of telling Ellie what she doesn't know, when the zipper on Ceo's tent goes up. Grahame sticks his head out, surveys the day.

Ellie hisses to me, "Don't leave me alone with him, *Ever.* Promise?"

"I promise."

"Say it."

"I promise not to leave you alone with Grahame."

She reaches out and squeezes my hand. Then says in her normal voice as Grahame walks up to the fire, "Well, Colin. It looks like the snow has melted."

63

ELLIE

Looking down at the steaming pot, Grahame says, "What's for breakfast, Q?"

"Water. For our search. We'll get more at the creek."

"Good thinking. Did the Slim Jims make you thirsty?"

"Pack up your stuff. I want to leave in five minutes."

"I'm packed already. All we need to do is take down the tent."

"Good. Then do it."

Ignoring Colin, he says to her, "How was your night in the fort?"

"We survived."

"I noticed." While she keeps her eyes on the flames, he adds, "I hear skin on skin is the best way to get warm. All the friction. Is that true?"

She stares at the fire.

Grahame says, "Must be. You've got that nice survivor's glow."

She raises her eyes, glares at him. Grahame's eyes flick to the ax, then back to her. It's a subtle thing. Colin probably missed it.

Colin says, "Grahame, break down the tent."

"I be on it, boss mon." And walks away.

Ellie waits till he's inside the tent before turning to Colin.

"Something's different about him."

"Yeah, there is. He went through hell yesterday."

"I think he's losing it."

"He'll be okay."

She looks at Colin. "You told him?"

"Told him what?"

"How I feel about him."

Colin frowns, as if considering different answers to the same question. She's afraid he'll pick the lie and say no, Grahame has no idea. But Colin says, "I didn't tell him you think he's lying. But he basically said that to my face last night." Her heart sinks at Colin's tone, somewhere between disappointment and frustration. Maybe even a hint of anger. She was hoping for something different. That Colin would say he agrees with her, that he's on her side. Instead he hands her the empty water bottle and asks her to hold it while he pours in the pot of warm water. She has another coughing fit and spills some. When they're finished, he tells her to drink a little, maybe it will help her throat. She pauses, not feeling right about it.

Colin says, "Go ahead. We're way past worrying about cooties."

He disappears into the shelter, hands out their packs. By the time they put them on and tighten the straps, Grahame is finished breaking down the tent and joins them by the fire. They kick snow on the flames till nothing remains except a thin trail of smoke.

Colin says to Grahame, "It's your deal now."

They stare at the untracked snow. The only sound being the soft thump of branches shedding their heavy load.

Colin reaches for the ax. Grahame beats him to it. Then he turns to Ellie and says, "He was my friend, too. It was an accident." Waits for an answer that doesn't come. He points the handle of the ax into the woods and says, "Me tink we go dat way, don't cha know."

Grahame leads, Colin trails a few steps back. Ellie looks over her shoulder at the shelter that she built with Colin. Remembers the feel of his arm wrapping around her chest, pulling her to him. The promise of warmth it brought in the middle of a storm. She recalls what Colin said this morning when she asked if they should tear it down.

It was good to us. Let's leave it up.

Ellie smiles at that thought, then leans over and coughs.

Colin looks back, concerned.

She says, "I'm all right." Then follows his tracks into the woods.

64

COLIN

We walk in a silence occasionally broken by my calling out Ceo's name and Ellie's coughing, which is progressively worse. Water doesn't help. She refuses to rest or to go back to the shelter and wait. So here we are.

Grahame stops every couple minutes, looks around, shakes his head, and moves on, but not without giving me a glare that makes it perfectly clear what he thinks of our weary parade. Staying in his tracks is a challenge because his strides are longer than mine. I keep stumbling, which takes its toll on my strength as I struggle to stay upright with this load on my back. A hiking stick would help. I keep an eye out for something that will work.

After we've been at it for thirty minutes, Grahame stops and says, "Q, this is insane."

"Keep going."

"How long are we going to do this?"

"We'll stop when we find him."

"Have you thought about what we're going to do if that happens?"

"What do you mean?"

"He's dead. We can't carry him."

"What if he isn't dead?"

"We should be hiking out of here, Q. That's what we should be doing."

I know he's right. But I can't stop. Not until I'm sure.

I ask, "Does anything look familiar?"

Grahame snorts. "It was a blizzard, Q. Nothing looks familiar."

Ellie says, "Colin. Maybe we should set a time limit."

Grahame says, "Yeah. A time limit. I vote for that."

They look at me. I know we can't keep this up indefinitely. All we've had to eat are a couple of Slim Jims. It's a race to see which we run out of first, calories or water. We still have to find the trail and hike out of here. The weather won't hold, and when it changes, we won't have the energy to fight it. I know they're right.

I ask, "How much time is Ceo worth?"

Grahame starts to reach into a coat pocket, changes his mind, and switches to his pants pocket. He comes out with his phone. "It's eight forty-two now. I say we turn around at nine. No matter what."

"That's it? Ceo's life is worth eighteen minutes?"

"Considering that this pointless search could kill us all, I say hell yeah."

Ellie says, "Colin. We can't keep doing this. I'm sorry."

Grahame says to her, "You and I could head down. Let Colin do this on his own."

I'm tempted to agree. Then I remember my promise to Ellie. That I won't leave her alone with Grahame. I say, "All right. Ceo gets eighteen minutes. Let's go."

Grahame resumes kicking postholes in the snow. We follow in a tight line behind him. After a couple minutes he says, "Hey, Ellie. Did Q tell you about the big match?"

Right away I don't like the sound of this. Whatever cliff he's headed for, it can't be good. I say, "Grahame, don't. Not now."

"C'mon, Q. Might as well tell her. It's the whole reason we're out here, right?"

"What do you mean? What match?" Ellie says.

Grahame's laugh echoes across the snow. "Seriously? With all the alone time you two have had, Q hasn't told you about how Ceo, his *BFF*, cratered his scholarship?"

Ellie says, "Colin, you had a scholarship to CGA?"

"'Had' is the right tense."

"I didn't know prep schools gave out athletic scholarships."

"Technically it was a student-athlete grant. It was funded by the local tennis patrons association, not the school. They award two every other year. A kid transferred out. I applied and got lucky."

Grahame says, "In order for Q to get the scholarship—excuse me, *grant*—he had to keep his grades up and stay in the top two spots on the team. Since I'm basically unbeatable, the number two spot was his only hope. Coach schedules challenge matches between players in the fall to determine the top eight when the season starts in the spring. He and Ceo had played two matches and were tied, one to one."

"Grahame, let's focus on Ceo, okay? He's—"

"Ceo isn't going anywhere. Trust me." He looks at his phone. "You've got twelve minutes left. Goalie girl needs to know why we're tromping around in this miserable fucking forest." As if responding to him, a nearby tree takes a dump by shedding a load of snow. It thuds softly ten feet to our left. Grahame starts walking again. He says, "So Q is playing Ceo for the tiebreaker match. The winner gets to challenge me for the number one spot. Ceo wants to beat me more than anything. But Q's playing out of his mind. He's crushing Ceo. I'm playing on the court next to them, watching Ceo get more and more pissed. I'm thinking, Yeah, Q. Beat his ass." Grahame stops to examine some tracks in the snow, then continues down a short easy slope.

Ellie says, "Can you move this along?"

Grahame says, "Now it's match point. Colin comes to the net; Ceo hits a passing shot. Q makes the right call, and says it's out. Colin wins. But Ceo goes absolutely bat-shit. He calls Q a cheater, screams and yells. Smashes his racquet on the court, flings it so far it lands on the roof of the PE building." He pauses. "Now it's your turn, Q. Tell her what happened next."

I say, "There's nothing to tell."

Grahame says, "Ha! What happened is that Q did what everyone always does. He caved to Ceo and replayed the point. Double-faulted. Lost the game, then tanked the rest of the match. Ceo won. Q dropped to number three. Good-bye, grant."

"That's awful. Colin, can you appeal?"

"No. The board made it very clear when I accepted the grant. The athletic funding stays with the position, not the player. It's been like that for forty years. They said I'll still get the academic funding, but that isn't enough. Coach talked to the CGA board. They said all the aid packages are already assigned for this academic year."

Ellie says, "Why did Ceo do this to you?"

"He didn't. I did it to myself."

Grahame says, "Bullshit. Ceo's had a hard-on for beating me ever since I transferred in. This year is, make that *was*, his last chance. Poor Q was in his way."

"So all this is an ego thing?"

"Pretty much."

"And I thought ODP soccer was cutthroat." She coughs, hacks something up.

I stop, offer her some water. She takes a few sips, then says, "So what are you going to do?"

"Go back to Vermont, finish my senior year. Live with my mom and work. Save up some money, then probably go to Castleton."

Grahame says, "Hey, maybe after this shakes out, your situation on the team might, you know . . . improve."

I can't believe he said that. I say through clenched teeth, "He's still alive."

Grahame looks at his phone. "Yeah? For about seven minutes." Then, after twenty steps of blessed silence he says, "Ellie, you ever heard of kittens in a blender?"

And there's the cliff. That's where he's been headed all along. What will it take to shut him up? Measuring the closing distance from me to him, I hiss, "Grahame. Not another fucking word."

But Ellie doesn't answer his question. I don't hear her walking behind me.

Grahame says, "Ceo knows he did a shitty thing to Q. So he decides he's going to fix it by—"

Ellie says, "Hey, didn't you say there were two trees that made a V?"

65

ELLIE

The log is barely visible under the snow. But the branches, crooked and moss covered, rise up to shoulder height. They make her think of spider legs, upside-down and dead. She doesn't like this spot, this small clearing in the woods. It feels darker than it should. As if light is not welcome here. The snow is smooth, undisturbed. At peace. There is no hint of the violence that happened yesterday, other than a creeping sense of unease. There are no lumps on the surface suggesting a body underneath.

They shed their packs, lean them against the tree.

Grahame stands close to the branches, ax in hand.

Colin yells, "Ceo!" He waits. "Ceeeee-oooohhhh!"

Silence.

Ellie thinks: There isn't even an echo here.

Grahame says, "I was standing like this. Ceo was right there." He points to a spot six feet behind him. "Then I swung like this." He unshoulders his ax and moves it in a slow horizontal arc that starts low, ends high. In her mind she sees Ceo's head spinning sideways from the impact. Hears the blade slicing through skin, shattering bone. Teeth and blood splaying in the wind.

But there is no sound except her pounding heart.

And Grahame's feet sinking into snow as he moves two strides back.

"He landed about here, then fell backward to . . . here. This is where he should be." Grahame starts kicking the snow. Colin joins him. They move randomly, stomping down to dirt, churning the snow into cottage cheese.

Grahame says, "C'mon, Ceo. Where are you? Where are you?"

Colin falls to his knees, starts digging with his hands. Grahame does the same.

She feels a swelling in her throat, pressing from the inside out. Ellie knows she should not be here, that she is standing on the shadow of something, *someone*, that no longer exists. But she falls to the snow and digs with them. It is better than listening to the silent scream in her head.

After a couple minutes of this, Grahame stands. He looks at them, stunned. His eyes wide in disbelief.

Colin says, "Why are you stopping?"

"Because he isn't here."

"I thought you said he was dead."

"I know. But . . . but he isn't here."

Colin returns to digging, moving forward an inch at a time. His hand flies up, a clump of colored snow lands to his right. He stops, picks it up. There is something odd about its shape and hue. Dark, but not quite black. Maybe dark red. Dense, like ice. He studies it, turning it slowly in his hand. Then he looks down at where he is in the snow. Digs some more and comes up with another lump of stained ice. Then another. Her stomach tightens. Colin struggles to his feet. "This is blood," he says, throwing his discovery at Grahame. "Right here. Right where I'm standing. You said he died. Why isn't there a body?"

Grahame shakes his head, muttering words to himself. Colin walks toward him, stops six feet away. About the same distance, she thinks, that Ceo was from Grahame's swing. She's still kneeling a few feet behind Colin.

Colin says, "I'll tell you why there isn't a body. Because Ceo was alive."

"But he didn't have a pulse."

"Your fingers were too numb to feel a pulse."

"He had a convulsion. He stopped breathing."

"You couldn't hear breaths. Not in that wind."

"He was dead, Q. Deal with it."

She hears a wavering note in his voice that wasn't there before. *Is he as confused as we are?*

"Ceo was alive when you left him," Colin says. "That's the only way this works. You hit him with your follow-through. It was a mistake. You saw what you did and panicked. I get that. But now he's lost and he's hurt. We have to find him."

Grahame stares at Colin, his body tense, vibrating.

Ellie stands, moves next to Colin.

And it starts to rain. Drops at first, making small holes in the snow. Then *hard*.

She chokes back a cough. Says to Grahame, "You know it wasn't a mistake."

His eyes shift to her. "You weren't there. You don't know."

"You've been looking for a way to get back at Ceo ever since he beat you in that race."

Back to Colin, he says, "She's your girl. Tell her to shut up."

She's your girl? This fuels the rage billowing inside her.

She says, "No. You're going to own up to this. You told him to stand behind you. Just like you told me to stand behind you. Then swung your ax and hit him."

"I slipped," he says. "I missed the branches and—"

"The only thing you missed is his *neck*."

Grahame takes a step toward her. She catches a movement—his fingers twitching on the handle of the ax.

"Ellie," Colin says, moving forward slowly, as if to stand in front of her. "Don't do this. It was a mistake."

Grahame says, "She stepped on da court, mon. Eets time to play. So what happened next, goalie girl? If I killed him, then where's the *fucking body?*"

"Don't answer him," Colin says.

She knows he's right. She should stop here, not say another word. Let them settle it without her. But there's something about the defiant look on Grahame's face that keeps her pressing. Even if he has an ax in his hand. She says through the pounding rain, "You dragged him off somewhere! You hoped the snow would bury him—"

Grahame's eyes go wide. She sees them filling with fear.

"That's it," he says to her. "That's what happened." He turns to Colin, his voice shaking. "It was the bear!"

"The *what?*"

"The bear. It smelled his blood. He came here in the night and dragged Ceo away. His body's in a cave somewhere. We'll never find what's left of it." Grahame's eyes flick from Colin to Ellie and back again.

Colin says, "Grahame. This is crazy. You can't possibly believe—"

"No! Listen to me. I'm not crazy. That bear has been stalking us the whole time. You know it has. It was six inches from your head. First it ate our food. Now it's tasted human flesh. Once that happens . . . oh shit. We have to get out of here!"

Ellie says, "God, you're so full of it." But she knows the fear in his eyes is not for show. It's as real as the bloody snow at their feet.

Grahame moves to go past them. Colin reaches out to stop him. "We have to keep looking. You can't just leave him."

He rams Colin in the chest with the head of the ax. Knocks him backward. Colin falls into the snow, clutching his chest, gasping for air. Ellie is frozen by the sudden violence, the power. Grahame lunges at her, grabs her coat, and tosses her aside. She goes down. Ellie tries to scuttle backward. The snow is too deep, too wet. It's like falling into fresh concrete. He straddles her, his face twisted with rage and stone-cold fear. "It was the bear," he says. "If you can't figure that out, then you deserve to be his next meal."

He starts to raise the ax. She tries to twist sideways, to avoid the inevitable blow.

Colin with a roar slams into him. Knocks Grahame sideways. He staggers but doesn't go down. Colin slides between them, taking short, ragged breaths. Grabbing Grahame's chest with one arm. Ellie struggles to her feet. Grahame faces Colin, the ax up and ready. It looks like a stick in his powerful arms.

Colin says, "Go. Get out of here. I don't want to see your lying face ever again."

Grahame slowly lowers the ax. He turns and puts on his pack. Then wipes at the blood streaming from his nose with the back of his glove. "Ceo is right about one ting, mon," he says, eyes on Ellie. "You two deserve each other."

And runs past them, down the slope.

66

COLIN

The pounding rain.

It falls around us from a solid roof of gray. I know this kind of sky. It doesn't belong to a storm that comes and goes, that tears things apart, buries it all, and leaves in a hurry. This is the kind that settles in. Gets comfortable. It stays and stays until the world below is beaten down and weary. I also know that it's rain now, but how long will that last? We're probably in the upper thirties. That could turn to snow in a heartbeat. Wet is one thing. Cold and wet is another. The good news, at this moment anyway, is we can see far enough to get a sense of where we are. A confirmation of that sense would help. I reach for the map in my back pocket. It's not there. I think for a moment, then I remember why.

Ellie says, "What's wrong? Besides the obvious, I mean."

I say nothing.

"Colin?"

"Ceo has the map."

"Oh."

I scan the trees. A mist is rising as the warmer rain hits the snow.

"We won't last long in this," I say.

"What are our options?"

I take it all in, the tree with the branches, the clearing where Ceo was supposed to be but is not. The endless contours of white that could be hiding him. I picture him sitting down, slumped over, back to a tree. I think of Ellie, wet and shivering, coughing longer and harder. I do a mental inventory of what we have left. Grahame took his pack. He has the tent, rain fly, the biggest water bottle, the matches, the ax. He has any hope we have of making a shelter and being dry. We have two sleeping bags, one of them wet, Ceo's Gore-Tex shell, and two foam pads. That's not enough to survive in what Mother Nature is doing to us now. And it could get worse.

"We're going to leave," I say.

"What about Ceo?"

"We have to get down today."

"Could we stay in the lean-to?"

I think about that. "We can't risk this rain turning into snow. Plus with this rain, we probably can't start a fire. It's time to do something about our situation." I choke on the words I'm about to say. "Ceo's on his own."

Ellie moves in close to me. I wrap my arms around her. There isn't time for this, but it's something we both need.

"I'm so sorry," she says.

"He's still alive," I tell her. "I know it."

We consolidate the two packs into one. Leave our wet clothes behind. Only carry the essentials. I shoulder the pack—and am instantly stabbed by a sharp, burning pain in my chest where Grahame hit me. He probably broke some ribs. Ellie sees this, offers to carry the pack. I tell her I'm good for now, that all we have to do is make it to the switchbacks, then we can drop the pack. She's okay with this plan. The hard reality is we both know she's sick and will need all the energy she has for the descent.

We stand for a moment, considering the best direction to go. Our goal is the same as when Ceo led us down off the mountain—find Snow Creek, follow it to the footbridge, and cross, then work our way to the rim. Finding the trail from there should be easy. Walking down those switchbacks in my wet sneakers will be another challenge, but I put off that worry for later.

Ellie says, "Should we follow Grahame's tracks?"

"He's headed in the right direction."

She takes a few steps. I ask her to stop.

I cup my hands to my mouth and yell, "CEEEEEEEEE-OHHHHHHHHHHHH!"

We wait ten empty seconds.

"Let's go," I say.

The rain just won't let up. It sinks into the snow and turns the bottom two inches into a layer of slush that sticks to everything. Each step is heavier than the one before it. I suppose I should be thankful there isn't any wind. I keep reminding Ellie that it took us about an hour to hike from the valley rim to our campsite on the first night. So this ordeal can't go on much longer. That logic seemed believable at first. Now I don't know. We continue to follow Grahame's trail, which is helpful. Sometimes we a spot a spray of blood where he stopped to clear his nose. Other than that, there's been no sign of him.

Ellie slows to a stop and says, "I need to rest."

I point to a snow-covered boulder about ten feet away. "We can sit there."

We walk together to the rock. I brush off the snow and we sit hunched over, side by side. She's shivering in convulsive waves. I decide to risk the pain and take off my pack. I dig out Ceo's Gore-Tex bivy sack, unzip it, drape it over our heads and shoulders. At least that slows the rain a little.

She says, "Thanks."

"We're almost in the end zone," I say.

Ellie smacks my arm with her elbow.

"What's that for?"

"*We're almost in the end zone?* That was a serious violation of the no-sports-metaphor clause."

"But I'm hypothermic. I can't feel my feet."

"Are you appealing the ruling?"

"I am. It is unjust."

"Let me check with the judges." After a moment, "They say there is no excusing a metaphor that bad. The ruling stands."

I smile. So Ellie's brain is working okay. That's good.

Then she coughs. Spits out a gob of green spotted with red.

"Sorry to be so gross," she says. "I've decided I'm not a good snow camper."

"From now on, I say we stick to sand camping. Leave this cold white stuff for the penguins."

We listen to the rain tapping over our heads. Watch the mist rise up as if trying to escape the gathering moisture below. The world up here has turned into a giant sponge. And it's full.

Ellie says, "Ceo told me something in the tent. I want to know how much of it is true."

Here it comes. *Ceo's revelation*. I thought we had left this cloud behind. I say, "Considering the source, probably not much."

"It's a long list."

"Go ahead. I'm listening." I brace myself, wondering if it's possible to get colder than I already am.

"He said he did something to you that he wishes he could undo. That you're his best friend and that he loves you like a brother. He said he would ask you to be his best man in all six of his future weddings. That you're a better friend than he deserves, and if I let you go, I'll be cursed for a thousand lives."

It takes me a moment to recover. *If I let you go*. I like that.

"That's a pretty good list," I finally say.

"How much of it is true?"

"All of it. Except that part about being cursed for a thousand lives. That's excessive."

"Good answer."

I feel warmer than I did a minute ago.

She says, "Now for my follow-up question. Who's your favorite cinematographer?"

"After you?"

"Of course."

"That would be no one."

Smiling at me, she says, "The judges are happy."

And right there, on this cold wet rock in the middle of an unforgiving wilderness, we kiss. It's only for a moment. Three heartbeats, maybe four. Then we pull apart, and she coughs and coughs. I rub her back under the tarp, pondering that moment and how the rest of this day in the presence of that moment seemed to disappear.

After she settles I say, "I like this rock. It has magical powers. We should visit again when it's warmer."

"I'd like that."

"But now we should go."

"I'm not ready yet. Give me another minute. Besides, I have one more question to ask."

"Okay."

"What did Grahame mean by 'kittens in a blender'?"

I take a deep breath. It goes all the way down to my frozen feet. Since there isn't time to get around it, I head straight for the truth. "Ceo did a stupid thing. He put this trip together because he wanted me to meet you."

"Meet? As in Colin, this is Ellie? Or, Colin, here's Ellie. You two should hook up."

"More like the second part. He thought it would make up for what he did at the challenge match."

"So I was your consolation prize?"

"On his planet, not mine."

"Were you a part of this plan?"

"Not willingly."

"What about Grahame?"

"He overheard Ceo tell me when we were calibrating the GPS." She makes a strange sound, not quite a cough. Like she's swallowing an ache. I look for her eyes. She avoids me. I say, "You should also know that's when Ceo told me something happened the night before in the tent. He said I blew my chance. That he was falling for you, hard."

I hear that sound again. Feel her shaking beside me. Then after a long beat, "You're right. We should go."

We stand. I stuff the bivy sack into my pack, slip it over my shoulders, wince at the searing pain. She returns to Grahame's tracks, starts following them to who knows where.

I say as the rain falls, "The contestant from Vermont wants to know. Are the judges still happy?"

She says without turning around, "They're conferring."

67

COLIN

We continue to follow Grahame's tracks. They're starting to meander more, which worries me. His physical state is probably no better than ours. I feel like we're moving in a direction that is more parallel to the creek then designed to intersect it. I'm thinking it's about time to start breaking our own trail when Grahame's tracks take a sharp turn to the right. This feels like a better course, but I'm still nervous. We can't afford to make mistakes. Not even one. I decide to give it five minutes. If nothing changes, then I'll suggest we take a more direct line in the direction of what I believe to be west, toward North Dome.

About one hundred yards into our march, Ellie stops again. This time she tilts her head, holds up her hand for me to be quiet. A few seconds later she says, "Do you hear that?"

"What am I supposed to hear?"

"Straight ahead." She points in the direction of Grahame's tracks. "In the trees."

I'm thinking she hears some kind of animal, like a deer or maybe the alleged bear.

Or Grahame.

She asks, "Is it the wind?"

This time I know what sound I'm listening for.

And I hear it. A low whispering rush. Something moving fast. It could be a wind stirring up. That would be very bad news. The last thing we need is wind. But I don't see any branches moving. The patches of mist remain low and undisturbed. I take a few steps closer to the source—and then I know what it is.

Water.

It takes us ten minutes of hard slogging, and costs us nearly every remaining calorie we have, but we make it to the creek. My first thought is this can't be the same creek. It's not the bubbling little trout stream my father would love to fish on a Sunday afternoon. This one is too big, moving too fast. There's no way we can cross it without a bridge. I try to picture the map in my head—I don't remember any other streams in this area. The only explanation I can think of is this is what Snow Creek looks like after twelve hours of relentless rain, followed by a foot of wet snow, followed by even heavier rain with temps significantly above the freezing mark.

Ellie points to Grahame's prints. They split, one heading upstream, the other down. He must have been wondering the same thing I am. Are we above the bridge, or below it?

"Wait here," I tell her. "I'm going to follow the tracks upstream for a little ways. See if Grahame found the bridge."

She shakes her head, then bends over coughing. I stand there, helpless, till she stops. Ellie wipes her mouth with her glove. "I'm not waiting here alone," she says.

I'm too tired to argue, and I know she's right. We head upstream together. The going gets hard in a hurry. Lots of fresh blowdowns from the storm, rocks to negotiate and too many places where my sneakers are likely to slip. I'm also worried about a few spots where the high water seems to be undercutting the banks. I saw the snow break away twice, with big chunks falling into the current. We can't ignore the possibility that we're above the bridge, which means continuing in this direction is a waste of time and resources we don't have. Apparently Grahame arrived at the same conclusion—this is too difficult and dangerous. His tracks stop. So do ours.

We turn around.

68

ELLIE

On the way back she wants to hear him talk. To help her keep her mind off the burning ache in her chest every time she coughs. She is cold and hot at the same time. Knows that she has a fever and it is getting worse. They're far enough from the roar of the water now.

She asks, "Why are you so sure Ceo is alive?"

He helps her over a fallen tree, then says, "Ceo gave me a ride to the airport on the day my father died. It was a red-eye, so we had a little time to play at the beach. After two hours of body surfing and playing Frisbee football all up and down the beach, it was time for me to catch my flight. When we get to the car, Ceo realizes he has a hole in his shorts. The keys are gone. Our cell phones and wallets are in the trunk. There isn't anyone around. It's dark. All he has is moonlight to see. I'm thinking it's game over. I'm going to miss the flight. Ceo says not to worry, he'll find the keys, and he takes off. I watch him run up and down the beach. Head down, arms flailing. As if he can actually do this impossible thing. I'm already thinking about how I'm going to tell my mom that I missed the flight—when Ceo walks out into the waves, bends down to pick something up. And guess what?"

Ellie notices that they're back to the spot where the tracks split. Colin keeps moving, this time in the other direction, downstream.

She says, "Don't tell me Ceo found the keys."

"He absolutely did. I made it to the airport just in time to catch my flight."

"Finding keys in the sand is not the same thing as getting axed in the head in the middle of a blizzard."

"True. But there is one point where they are the same. Ceo, against all odds, believed he would find those keys. I wouldn't have even tried. And I'm certain he would believe that he can find a way to survive. Most people give up. I would. But Ceo is like this storm. He's a force of nature."

She considers everything she's learned about Ceo since she met him. Remembers how he charmed her at the airport into riding with them as far as the gate. How he convinced Grahame into carrying that rock. He knew what to say and when to say it. She decides that Colin is right—Ceo is a force of nature. But then she remembers Grahame and the sheer force of the ax when he hit that tree.

Nature doesn't always win.

They round a small bend and see a lump in the snow about ten feet from the bank. As they get closer she knows what it is. Grahame's pack. He stopped at a tree that must have been blown down by the storm, carried by the current to this place, where it got stuck between the banks. Thick and with roots at the near end. Angling down slightly and more narrow at the far end. She figures the distance is thirty feet. It has branches rising up out of the current. Most are dead, but a few are still green. Water flows over the last ten feet. It's hard to tell how deep. Maybe six inches, but it could be more. The bank on the opposite side is rocky and steep.

Colin slides off his pack. He says, "Grahame made it across. I see his tracks on the other side."

She says, "There has to be a better way."

"I doubt it. His tracks keep going downstream. Something made him come back and cross here."

"Please. Find a better way." Then she coughs until it feels like her lungs are coming up in pieces through her throat. Colin holds her while she settles, then gives her a sip from his water bottle. It's the same one they filled this morning. After that night in the lean-to. That was the last time she was warm. She closes her eyes and wishes she were there.

Then she looks at that tree spanning the current and thinks: I wish I was anywhere but here.

Colin says, "Can you wait here while I check downstream?"

Ellie hesitates.

He says, "Grahame is on the way down. He isn't a threat."

She says, "Go. But you better come back."

69

COLIN

I stare at the reason Grahame crossed at the tree. A short distance away the water dips down, bends slightly to the left, down a bit more, then disappears. I hear the muted rumble of water crashing on the rocks below. Remember seeing it on the way up. A thick ribbon of white with a shower of spray at the base.

Snow Creek Falls.

By the time I get back to her, Ellie is sitting on Grahame's pack, hunched over and shivering. But her face is blazing red. I feel her cheek with the back of my hand. Even through the cold and wet, I can tell she's on fire.

"You have a fever," I say.

She nods. "Anything better downstream?"

I hesitate, not sure how this news will hit her. But she needs to know. "The falls," I say.

After a moment Ellie closes her eyes. I'm sure she just went through the same thought progression I did. That if we had followed the creek instead of turning around like Grahame did, we would have hit the bridge. We'd be on the other side by now, working our way down the switchbacks. Instead we're faced with backtracking two miles, half of it uphill. Meanwhile her fever gets worse and the rain continues to beat us down and down.

She looks at me and says, "I just don't have it in me to go back."

"I could—" And then it hits me. I can't believe I didn't think of it before. Filled with a rush of hope, I ask, "Where's your cell phone? Didn't you get reception up here?"

"It's in the pack."

"Where? Which pocket?" I pick up my pack.

She shakes her head. "The *other* pack. The one we left behind."

"Shit! Why didn't you tell me?"

"I remembered while you were gone. I checked all the pockets. It's not here. We'd just been through that thing with Grahame. It was raining. . . . I hadn't used it in so long. . . . I forgot. I'm so sorry."

"It's all right. Knowing our luck it wouldn't work anyway."

I look at the tree. At Grahame's footprints tempting us, thirty feet away. Then I look at his pack, consider the contents and how best to use it.

"What are you thinking?" she asks.

"If hiking to the bridge is out, then we have three options. Option one is I set up the tent and you wait inside in Ceo's sleeping bag. I'll cross the log and go for help. It would probably take me a couple hours to get down. Give it another hour to walk the Mirror Lake Trail and find help. Option two is we wait here and hope Grahame tells someone about us, or that someone is missing us and calls the park. Option three is we cross that log, head down the trail together. That's the way I see it. It's your call."

"I don't want to be left alone."

"That rules out option one."

"I'm sorry, but I don't trust Grahame. We're witnesses to his crime. He won't tell anyone about us. And Ceo filled out a permit for a different place. I lied about where I was going, and so did you. No one will look for us up here."

"I trust Grahame to make the call. You're wrong about that. But we'll rule out sit and wait."

"So that leaves us with the log."

Right or wrong, that's where we are. I say, "Grahame did it. In his giant clown feet. You'll have more tree to stand on than he did."

"What about you? In those sneakers? You said you can't feel your feet."

"I'll be okay. There are lots of branches to hold on to. Plus here's a fun fact. They called me 'balance boy' in high school. I can balance a cucumber on the tip of my finger. It's one of my special talents."

She manages a weak smile. "You're not the only one with talents. I was in gymnastics before I played soccer. Balance beam was my specialty."

"So you can do a back handspring with a full dismount. We've got this."

"Okay," she says, sitting up. Her voice taking on a confident edge. "Who goes first?"

"I should. That way I'm on the other side and can help you. The only real tricky part is the last ten feet." Actually that's a bald-faced lie. The whole thing looks tricky to me. The log could be icy. It could move. There's a big branch in the way. Getting around it won't be easy. If we fall, there is no swimming to the other side. The more I think about it, the less I like it. Ellie's sick and weak.

And she's right about my feet; they're worthless bricks. Sit and wait is looking pretty good to me.

She says, "I'm worried that if you get over there first, I may be too afraid to go. Then I'll be left alone. So I'm going first."

"What if you have a coughing fit?"

"I'll just have to not let that happen." She stands. "Let's cross that bridge, *balance boy*."

70

ELLIE

They walk down to the tree. Feel the surface. The bark is wet but not icy. He tries to shake it. No movement.

Colin says, "It's in there good." He gives her a hug. Pulls back, looks at her, and says, *"Your assault on the world begins now."*

Despite it all, she manages a smile. "John Cusack as Lloyd Dobler, *Say Anything*, 1989. That's the movie that made me fall in love with him."

"See! Your mind is working great. You can do this, Ellie. Use the branches. If you do fall, try to fall upstrea—"

"No more talking, okay?" she says. "Your helping is not helping."

Ellie climbs up onto the log. She stands for a moment, tries to forget the deafening roar of the water, the icy current sliding underneath and over. Fights off the fear of what would happen if she falls. Waits to get balanced, starts moving forward one foot in front of the other. After about fifteen seconds she is midstream and has to work her way around the first branch. There's still plenty of trunk to stand on. She gets around that, and the tree narrows considerably. She senses through her feet the vibration of the current surging against the wood. Hears Colin behind her saying, *You've got this, keep going.* Looking forward, she realizes the next branch is the point of no return. Get past that and there is no going back. She reminds herself to breathe. Five more steps. Turns slightly sideways, inches her feet slowly around the branch. Next up is the part where she gets wet. It's two feet away. She can't see the trunk, has to guess where the wood is. There's nothing to hold on to. Her heart is racing faster than the current. Her legs are starting to shake. Feels a cough coming on. Seconds from falling...

A voice, strong and confident and *very close* says, "I'm right here. Don't stop now."

Ellie glances up. Grahame. He's at the water's edge, boots inches from the current, reaching out with a big bare hand. She hesitates, wanting his help, afraid he'll do something that sends her into the water.

"C'mon, Ellie," he says. "I've got you. Don't you stop now."

She puts one foot out, feels for the wood that she can't see. The water is cold, icy cold. She slides out a little farther. Both feet are in the water. She's an arm's length from Grahame's steady hand. The current pushes at her, turns her sideways. She's starting to fall. Takes a quick step, then a desperate lunge for Grahame's hand. Strong fingers wrap around her wrist. He pulls her to him. She hits the other side and sprawls in the snow, gasping. It turns into a ragged cough.

Grahame says, "Nice job. Now get up there where it's safe. It's too slippery down here."

"How did you . . . I mean how . . ."

"Don't look so surprised. I knew you guys would follow my tracks. I was on my way down, but figured you might need my help getting over this tree."

"Thank you."

"No worries. Now get up there. I need to help Q. He's on his way."

She turns around. Colin is already at the first branch. He doesn't look solid. His arms are waving too much. He's moving too fast—*why is he doing that?* His lips are tight, face drawn. He glances at her. She sees fear. The unshakable kind, the fear of knowing a certain future and not being able to change it.

It's his feet, she thinks. He can't feel the wood.

Grahame shouts over the water, "Q. Turn around! We'll go for help!"

He shakes his head.

Then she realizes what's wrong. *He promised he wouldn't leave me alone.*

"All right, then," Grahame says. "Settle down. Relax. Breathe. You've got this. One foot in front of the other. Do it slow. . . ."

Colin settles, moves again. He gets around the first branch, starts to lean, waves his arms wildly, reaches back and grabs the top of the branch. He steadies, shakes his head. Twelve feet away. He looks at her again. The fear isn't quite as strong. Confidence is coming back.

She says, "Almost here, Colin."

Then Grahame says, "Oh *SHIT*!"

A second later a tree from upstream slams into the log. Colin looks at Ellie, eyes wide in disbelief. He twists, reaches out for a branch that isn't there.

His right leg slips off the log.

He falls into the current.

71

COLIN

The water is so damn cold. I struggle to breathe as the current presses against my back and rushes over me. I'm holding on to a branch that's slightly above the surface. I don't know how much longer I can do this. My fingers are numb. The current is pulling at my legs, trying to suck me under the tree and away. If there's a bottom down there, I can't feel it.

Grahame is yelling my name.

I look at them through the water streaming across my face.

Ellie is leaning out at an impossible angle, her body over the water. One arm is tied to Grahame's coat. It increases her reach by three feet. In her other hand is the ax. She's holding it out to me and having problems keeping it up. It's too heavy.

Grahame screams, "Grab the ax. Colin! Do it!"

It's just beyond my reach. To get there means letting go of the branch. If I do that, the current will take me under, and that's it for me. For a moment I think that might be a better result. Ellie is risking her life, and so is Grahame. If I let go, they're safe. But then Ellie would be left alone with Grahame. I can't let that happen. My strength is fading fast.

She screams, "Colin! Now!"

I let go of the branch. The current is on me like some huge underwater beast. It's clawing at my legs, pulling me down. I dig my fingernails into the bark with my right hand, reach out with my left. Slide forward an inch, then another. My fingers touch the ax. It's wet. They slip off at first, then with a final stretch, they wrap around the head of the blade. I feel another pull. But it isn't the current. It's Grahame and Ellie, hauling me to shore.

His arms grab mine. I feel rocks and ground below my legs. Something solid to stand on. I collapse back onto the snow. Ellie is beside me, coughing.

Grahame beams down at me.

"Dat was a hell of a ting, mon!"

He raises his arms in triumph.

I wrap my arms around Ellie. Close my eyes. She's crying.

Then I hear a short, sharp yell.

Look up.

The place where Grahame was standing is no longer white. The snow gave way below him. It was smooth rock underneath. I scan downstream. Spot an arm, his hat.

I scream, "GRAHAME! GRAHAME!"

The current is too fast.

He's around the bend and gone.

72

ELLIE

She sits beside him in the snow, up high with their backs against a tree, away from that awful sound of water thundering over rocks.

He's soaked and shaking with no way to get dry. Everything is cold. Every part of her.

Their packs are on the other side, taunting them. The log that slammed into their bridge knocked it loose. The closest end to them isn't reachable without swimming into the current. They'd be swept away, just like Grahame. They have no food, no way to make a fire. All they have is Grahame's jacket. It's wrapped around their shoulders, offering little comfort against the rain, which has somehow gotten worse. And now there's a wind. It is blowing from across the valley, biting into the rest of whatever life they have left. They've seen a few flakes mixed in. Snow is coming. Colin said a minute ago that they should build a shelter. But he couldn't even stand. And she can't walk ten feet without going into a coughing fit that ends with her spitting up blood.

He breaks their silence by saying through chattering teeth, "I'm sorry, Ellie. This is all so...so..."

"Messed up?"

"Grahame would use a stronger word."

"He came back for us."

"Yes, he did."

"You were right about him."

"We were both right," he says.

They shiver in silence. Then she hears what could be a laugh. "What's so funny?"

"So we're at a gas station. It's night. It's pouring rain. We're out of gas. Out of money. She says, 'I have a—'"

"'Credit card.'"

Colin says in a slightly lower voice, "'You have a credit card?'"

Ellie elevates her voice, "'Yes, but—'" She coughs hard, spits. "'My father told me to only use it in case of an emergency.'"

And she says with him, "'Well, maybe one will come up.'"

A jealous wind carries their laughter away.

Ellie says, "Your Cusack needs some work, buster."

"Maybe . . . that's because . . . my lips . . . are blue."

"Well, I thought my Daphne Zuniga was quite excellent."

"I agree. Hawking up the phlegm really nailed it."

They fall into another silence. She notes that they get longer each time. It takes too much effort to talk. Or think. She wonders how long it will take for the final silence to find them. The rain seems to have fallen off a bit, but not the wind. Ellie looks to her left, sees thick streaks of white mixing in. Flakes begin sticking to her wet pants. She coughs and says, "I heard it might snow today."

"Nah. That's just crazy talk."

She feels another silence coming on. Colin leans forward, pulls the coat a little tighter around them. A square bump rubs against her right arm. It's in a hidden pocket inside the lining.

Ellie finds the zipper, can barely manage the tab with numb fingers.

She pulls out... an iPhone.

They stare at it, not believing what she's holding in her hand. The face is covered with smears of dried blood.

"That's Ceo's," Colin says. "Please tell me it works."

Ellie pushes the home button. Nothing happens.

"Maybe it's turned off," Colin says.

Ellie finds and presses the power button. They stare in silence at the black face, hope fading with each passing second.

Colin says, "I guess we can toss—" and stops. The Apple symbol appears, then resolves into the home screen.

"Oh my God! It worked!" She kisses Colin on the cheek. "Two bars."

Colin laughs. "Like I told you. Ceo's a force of nature."

ALTA BATES SUMMIT MEDICAL CENTER
BERKELEY, CALIFORNIA

3 BACKPACKERS STRANDED BY STORM RESCUED, 1 DIES IN TRAGIC FALL

YOSEMITE, Calif. — A group of four backpackers, three from Los Angeles and one from San Rafael, California, were stranded in the wilderness for three nights by recent storms that hammered Northern California with 60 mph winds, record-breaking rain and up to two feet of snow at higher elevations. Yosemite Search and Rescue spokesperson Amanda Wilkes stated that the backpackers were reported missing by a friend in San Rafael Sunday night after one of the hikers missed her return flight from Fresno. High winds and near-zero visibility prevented rescue efforts until late Monday morning. Efforts were further hampered because the group filled out a wilderness permit for Lower Merced Pass Lake, but due to fires in that region, changed to the backcountry around Mount Watkins but failed to turn in a revised permit. Three of the four (Colin Tritt, 17, Ellie Boyer, 17, Ceo DeVrees, 18) were medevaced to a hospital in San Francisco, where they were treated for hypothermia and frostbite. DeVrees, who also suffered severe facial trauma, has been transferred to a hospital in Los Angeles. The fourth member of the party, Grahame Marcell, 18, was caught in a flash flood while attempting to cross Snow Creek and was swept over Snow Creek Falls. His body was recovered Monday night. An autopsy is pending.

SON OF MOVIE STUDIO EXEC SURVIVES AX BLOW TO HEAD IN WILDERNESS ORDEAL

BERKELEY, Calif. — Ceo DeVrees, 18, son of Christian R. DeVrees, CEO of Continental Development, Inc., and founder of Dancing Hippo Studios, was accidentally struck in the head with an ax by fellow hiker Grahame Marcell, 18, during a backpacking trip in Yosemite National Park. Believing the blow to be fatal, Marcell left DeVrees in a record-setting blizzard that dumped 6 inches of rain on San Francisco in 24 hours and up to 2 feet of snow in the Sierras. DeVrees managed to find the Snow Creek Cabin, which was occupied by a trail-maintenance crew weathering the storm. Marcell died the following day while attempting to cross Snow Creek in flash-flood conditions due to the storm. Park Ranger Nathan Row stated, "What this young man [DeVrees] did under those extreme conditions is a testimony to the sheer human will to

"'... survive. What's unfortunate in this—'"

"Please make it stop," Ceo says. "I've heard enough."

"Did you know about that cabin?"

"I read about it in the trail guide."

"Why didn't you tell us?"

"I wasn't sure which side of Watkins it was on. I didn't want to risk all of us trying to find it."

"So it was luck?"

"Pretty much. Except for the part where I got face-planted with a freaking ax."

The nurse told me I get ten minutes, then she needs to change his bandages. Hopefully, that gives me enough time to hear what I need to hear.

"Do you want these?" I show him the two clippings.

"What do you think?"

"I thought so. . . ." And I wad them up, toss them in the waste-basket under the TV. I settle back into the leather recliner next to his bed and force myself to look at him. To see if the Ceo I know is in this room. What I'm looking at is someone else. An IV is buried in his left arm. A gauze bandage is wrapped around the center of his head, covering his nose and cheeks, leaving the nostril holes open. One eye's swollen shut, the other's watery and discolored. A second bandage extends from his temple down to the jawline on the right side of his face. Any exposed skin from the neck up is puffy and varying shades of red, purple, and black. This is the first time I've seen him since the trip. Coach and Rhody visited him earlier today. Rhody said his face looks like he was dragged behind a train, then his remains were gnawed on by a pack of wolverines. I'd say for once Rhody didn't exaggerate.

I ask, "How long will you be Mummy Man?"

"They won't start the surgery until the swelling goes down. Then they'll slap on a chunk of flesh from my thigh. I'm going to be

Franken-Ceo for a while. But my dad is flying in a face doc from Germany. My agent says I have a very bright future modeling hockey masks." He nods at my crutches leaning against the chair. "How long are you on those?"

"Three weeks. Then I switch to a boot."

"Rhody told me you lost two toes."

"Actually only one. I don't consider the little guy a toe."

"Maybe this will solve your foot faulting problem."

"Yeah. But wearing flip-flops will be problematic."

"Right. Sorry about that."

I pause and say, "We all lost something."

His eye blinks. He swallows. A soft groan tells me pain is involved. A lot.

Ceo says, "When are you going back to school?"

"Monday. Coach got a hotel room about five blocks from here. I'm staying with him through the weekend. Rhody went back this morning. Ellie offered to let me stay at her house. We both decided that would be a little awkward."

Another pause. He asks, "How is she?"

I know Ellie hasn't been here to visit him. She says she has to work through some issues at home and in her head before that can happen. But she promised to visit before he leaves. I say, "She's good. Her lungs are clear. No digits lost. They released her two days ago."

"Tell her thanks for the card. It's by the TV, next to the *Scarface* DVD."

"*Scarface*? That sounds like Rhody."

"Worst get-well gift ever." Ceo smiles. At least I think it's a smile.

The nurse pokes her head in. "Five minutes to fresh bandage time." She winks at Ceo and closes the door.

"Her name is Claudia," Ceo says. "I call her Gauze-zilla."

It's time to put this conversation on a different course. I lean forward and say, "Your father told me you don't remember what happened."

He seems surprised at my question. I get a careful nod.

"Is that true?" I ask.

The eye narrows.

There's the Ceo I know.

He says, "I feel my memory coming back."

"Grahame told me it was an accident."

"I'm sure he did."

"Was it?"

"Before I answer your question, can you give me some water?"

There's a cup with a straw on his bedside stand, next to a pitcher of water. I fill the cup, give it to him. He takes a long pull through the straw, winces on the swallow. Then he closes his eye and says, "We were looking for the wood for your lean-to. Grahame kept chipping on me that all this is my fault. How stupid I was, how I lied to them. And he wouldn't stop going on about the GPS. Meanwhile you guys are freezing to death. I tell him to shut the hell up. He gets in my face. Says he knows that this whole trip is a setup. He knows about the kittens in the blender." His eye opens, focuses on me. "Did you tell him?"

"I didn't. He heard us when we were talking in the fog."

Ceo frowns at this piece of news. "I should've known he'd be skulking around. Anyway, I tell him we'll settle this later. He says, *You can fuckin' count on it.* A few minutes after that we find a log. It needs to be trimmed. I take a couple hacks at it. Grahame says this will take forever. He says give me the ax. So I give it to him. He tells me to stand behind him. I figure why not? It's gotta be safer than standing anywhere else. Then he takes this big swing at the branches. But he *misses.* I pull my head back just as the blade comes around."

Ceo takes a long pull on the straw. Says, "Dude, I need to stop talking. I've got a headache the size of Cuba."

I'd like to let him stop, but I'm not done yet. "He said he slipped. That's why he missed the tree."

"He didn't slip."

"Are you sure? All that snow?"

His voice goes hard. "He didn't slip."

I take a moment before saying, "What are you telling me, Ceo?"

"I'm telling you that if it were not for my catlike reflexes, he would've gone *Game of Thrones* on my skull."

This isn't making sense. The pieces aren't fitting right.

"If he was really trying to kill you," I say, choosing my words carefully, "then why didn't he finish the job?"

"I was thinking the same thing. So I faked a convulsion and acted like I was dead. There was so much blood in my mouth, that wasn't hard to do."

"What happened next?"

"He went through my pockets. Took my phone. Then he left."

"Did he feel for your pulse?"

"I honestly don't remember." Ceo takes a final sip, drains the glass, hands it to me. "I must've passed out after that. When I open my eyes, I'm covered with snow. It's almost dark. I have no clue where I am or what happened. I start walking and trying to call for help. It's kinda hard because my jaw is just a hanging flap of flesh. Eventually I see a light through the snow. You know how it rolls from there."

Neither one of us speaks. I stare at the IV bag, not wanting to think about what I just heard. I feel Ceo's eyes on me, even the one I can't see. There are muffled sounds outside the door.

I say, "There's one more question I have to ask."

"It better be short."

"If you're so sure Grahame wanted to kill you . . . why did you tell the police it was an accident?"

The door opens. The nurse sweeps into the room. She opens a drawer, pulls out a stack of bandages, some miscellaneous tubes and tape. She gives me the all-business glare, says it's time to go. I stand on my good foot, the one with five toes instead of three, and reach for my crutches.

Ceo says, "Q, I hear Grahame saved your life."

"He did," I say.

"That answers your question."

The nurse leans over Ceo's face. Peers down at him. Gently touches his skin with a gloved finger. He winces. She reaches behind his head, starts to unwrap the gauze. Says, "So a little bird told me your dad is in the movie business. . . ."

Yup, time to go. I heard what I came to hear, but I'm not sure it helped. I work my way across the room. Pause to look out the window at the city. As I reach for the door, Ceo says, "Hey, Q?"

"Yeah?"

"I told Coach."

"Told him what?"

My phone buzzes with a text, reminding me I have another place to be.

He says, "You made the right call. I cheated you out of that match."

I turn to face him. "When did you tell him?"

"That's the text I was sending when you guys picked me up in the parking lot at school. You're still number two. Your scholarship is reinstated."

Coach told me yesterday that I was funded through the end of the year. But he didn't say why. I thought it was because of the tragic change in our lineup. I like this reason better.

The nurse has a pair of tweezers in her hands. She says, "No more talking." Then slowly pulls back a quarter inch of gauze.

In the hallway, with Ceo's pain muffled by a closed door, I pull out my phone.

ELLIE

How is the force of nature?

COLIN

The same but with scars.

ELLIE

Did you hear what you needed?

Yes. How are the exploding heads?

I walk down the hall, stop at the elevator, press the down arrow.

Recovering. Where RU?

On my way down.

Shake a leg crutch boy. I don't want to miss the previews!

The elevator door opens. A nurse holding a cup of coffee in each hand smiles at me. I hobble in, thinking about who's waiting for me in the parking lot.

311

COLIN

Are the judges happy?

As the elevator door closes...

ELLIE

ACKNOWLEDGMENTS

I would like to thank my critique group for their bottomless patience and helpful feedback while I worked my way through the drafts. I'd like to thank my brother, Mike, for his extensive knowledge of hiking the backcountry of Yosemite. I'd like to thank Julie Rosenberg for seeing my vision and picking me. I'd like to thank my representation team, Doug Stewart and Chris George, for their unwavering support despite it all. And I'd like to thank my wife, Teresa, and son, Michael, for listening to my irrational concerns for four teenagers lost in an early snowstorm in Yosemite, one of my favorite places on the planet.